Dying To Go (Nothing to Gush About)
(A Tucson Valley Retirement Community Cozy Mystery)
By: Marcy Blesy

This book is a work of fiction. Names, characters, places, and events are a result of the imagination of the author or are used fictitiously. Any resemblance to actual persons, living or dead, businesses, events, or locations is a coincidence.

No part of the text may be reproduced without the written permission of the author, except for brief passages in reviews.

Copyright © 2023 by Marcy Blesy, LLC. All rights reserved. Cover design by Cormar Covers

Chapter 1

I should have mailed my belongings to Tucson. I'm losing the last bit of patience that remains, trying to get around boomers who crowd the moving carousel while I'm trying to retrieve two large, checked bags by myself.

I squeeze past a large gentleman with a PGA visor who is blocking my path when I see my flowered-cloth suitcase that Grandma Kate gave me when I graduated from high school. It's hard to believe that was over twenty years ago, and now I have a child that's graduated from high school, too. He'd only wanted money, though, nothing practical like luggage for all the adventures before him. This flowered piece of luggage has seen a lot of the world, from a posh boutique hotel in Paris to a camping site in the wilderness in Alaska to a seaside inn in Maine. I sigh, realizing that all of those trips had included Wesley who became my husband only to become *not* my husband.

My phone beeps. I pull it out of my pocket and check the message. It's Mom.

We're here. Where are you?

I type back my response only to realize I've missed my second bag. Crap! "Excuse me. Excuse me! Can someone please grab that black bag?" I move past a couple who are talking loudly, something about the value of having a fireplace in Arizona.

A row of eyes looks back at me like I'm crazy as a line of five or six black bags scoot along the luggage carousel. "Never mind. I'll wait." I drop my eyes and walk back to my old, tattered bag and wish I'd asked for something more practical like it instead of the trendy *everyone buys black luggage* that ended up on my wedding registry all those years ago. That had been Wesley's idea, of course. The luggage got split up during the divorce, too. I got the largest piece. He got the duffle bag and laptop bag.

"Ma'am is that your bag?" asks a young woman standing next to me as I'm reminiscing and regretting in my mind all at the same time.

"Oh, yes, thanks."

She smiles. I reach for my bag.

"Here, let me get that for you." Her husband, *boyfriend?* lifts my over-the-limit bag from the belt and sets it beside my other bag.

"Thanks," I say, before extending the handles of both bags and tugging them behind me. It seems as if everyone is arriving in Tucson today, probably others from the snowy Northern states like me, happy to see some sunshine.

"Ouch!" I hear from behind as I'm walking through the automatic doors. I turn around to see a middle-aged man who looks affronted and is pointing to his foot.

"Oh, sorry about that."

"Yeah, get some glasses, maybe?"

"I'll take that into consideration. Thanks," I say sarcastically.

"Rosi! Rosi! We are here!"

My mother is jumping up and down and waving her arms excitedly as she stands next to my parents' reliable Honda CRV. Dad had refused to buy something fun for himself in retirement, always the practical man, unlike many of his friends who had traded in practicality for a corvette or a refurbished '57 Chevy. "Hi, Mom."

Dad gets out of the car and insists on putting my luggage in the cargo area of the Honda though the whole reason I am here is to help out when he has his knee replacement surgery. The man can barely walk. "Hi, Rosi." He kisses me on the cheek after closing the door. "You are a sight for sore eyes," he whispers against my ear. "Your mother is driving me crazy."

"What are you two plotting?" Mom asks, grabbing my hand and pulling me to the car. "You take the front seat, Rosi. Dad will highlight attractions along the way."

Dad pats me on the knee as I take the front seat. His peppered hair is turning saltier by the year, and I touch my own brown hair, thankful that so far I've received Grandma Kate's genes and haven't started going gray. At almost forty, I have lots of friends who have been dying their hair for years. "The weather is sure nicer here this time of year than in Illinois."

"February is gorgeous in Tucson," Mom yells over the radio that is softly playing '70s classic rock as she leans forward between the two front seats.

"But there's no way you'd catch us here in the summer," says Dad. "They had twenty-five straight days last July in the three-digit temperature range. That's crazy!" He waves at a passing driver, the friendliest man I've ever known.

"We have so many plans, Rosi," says Mom. "You are going to love Tucson Valley."

"I'm not quite the demographic intended to love a retirement community, Mom."

"That's where you're wrong. There is so much to do! Plus, you're only a few years away from being able to rent a place here!"

I roll my eyes as I look out the side window at the barren landscape of the desert as we head out of Tucson and south of the city. "I'm 39."

"And at 55 you can rent your own place in Tucson Valley. It will be here before you know it!"

"Thanks for the encouragement."

"All I'm saying is that now that you are a divorcee with a kid in college, you have certain freedoms that you haven't had in the past. And maybe getting a place like we have in the desert in the middle of winter should be something to consider."

Dad turns to me and winks. "Just think, Rosi. We could be neighbors."

I smile to end this conversation. "That would be lovely." But what I really want to say is, *I'd rather eat dirt from a public park than live in a retirement community at 55 next door to my parents.*

Chapter 2

Mom has wasted no time in announcing to her friends at the Tucson Valley Retirement Community that I have arrived. I'd gone straight to bed last night after getting settled into my new room for a couple of weeks, or at least until Dad is fully mobile again, which hopefully won't be more than a few weeks. The house is nice. I can't deny that fact. It's only two bedrooms, but Dad's moved his amateur radio equipment off the desk in the spare bedroom he uses as an office so that I can have a workstation to edit stories for the digital edition of the Springfield Gazette and update social media, a shift away from writing the actual news stories in the capital city of Illinois. At least that's what my parents *think* I will be doing. I'm not ready for that conversation yet. The room also holds a queen-size bed, a dresser, and a nightstand. This might be the change I need after the year I've had.

The best part of the house is that it's on a hill that overlooks the hundreds of other houses that look the same but also with a view of the Santa Rita Mountains. I look forward to staring at the mountains while having my morning coffee. Otherwise, I'd be shoveling snow back home.

This morning, I'm awakened by the dinging of a spoon against what I can only imagine is a coffee mug from the clinking sound, probably her beloved Golden Girls coffee mug. I instinctively throw a pillow over my head, but the sound doesn't stop. Nor does my mother.

"Everyone will be here in an hour, Rosi. How about you take a shower and freshen up?"

"Okay, Mom. I'll get up. Give me a second."

"Rosi, your dad needs the bathroom for his morning business. He's on a schedule, you know. I think you need to take the shower while the bathroom's still open."

I throw the pillow off my head and sit up in bed, rubbing the sleep out of my eyes. Sharing a bathroom with my parents may prove more challenging than I'd considered.

"Great. And make sure to wear something cute," Mom says as she walks back out of the room. "Jan Jinkins has a nephew visiting next week, and I just know she's going to want to set you two up!"

"Mom! I don't want to be set up. I don't need to be set up!" But she's already back in the kitchen, jostling pots and pans in an effort to drown me out. Why couldn't

Simon take the responsibility of helping our parents? Why must it always be me? He's the one stuffing away wads of cash with all of his new tech start-ups, the latest idea being a "help me" app for senior citizens to get assistance with household chores. The problem is that most of the senior citizens I know can't figure out the app store, or at least they can't remember their passwords. The irony of my brother creating a senior citizen help app when *I'm* the one helping my parents is not lost on me. And somehow, he will manage to make money—lots of money. He always does. He's the golden child in our family. Everything he touches turns to gold: the perfect job, the perfect wife, the perfect looks, the perfect kids with number three having just been born—the first baby girl in the family—already being spoiled even though my parents have yet to see her. My sister-in-law Shelly had caved to Mom's insistence that they continue their annual tradition of visiting Tucson Valley before my parents leave, even though they live mere blocks away from each other in Illinois. Mom had relented to Shelly's request that the baby be a little bit older before they make the drive this spring.

  And here I am, Rosisophia Doroche, a conglomeration of the Golden Girls' names smushed together, mom's favorite show in the '80s, a most hideous name that I'd managed to keep a secret for all of my life until my mother filled out my high school graduation forms for my diploma. I didn't learn she'd done this until my name was called in front of my 120 high school classmates and their families before I walked across the stage for my diploma. The look of shock on my face is forever etched into the photos of that moment, and even the laughs and extra cheers have been captured on a video recording that I will never watch for any amount of money.

After showering and dressing in a light blue sundress and applying a bit of foundation, I wander into the kitchen where Mom is putting some sort of breakfast casserole into the oven. Mom turns to look at me, pausing in judgment as is her modus operandi. "Can't you apply a bit more makeup, Rosi? You're not a spring chicken anymore, you know?"

"Mom, I really don't think your friends will care if I've applied mascara." I grab an orange from the fruit basket on the table.

She swats my hand. "Save your appetite for breakfast. And Jan will care. It's her nephew that's coming to town next week for a visit. She needs to sell you, Rosi."

"*Sell me?* I'm not a horse. And I am not the least bit interested in dating."

Mom takes a deep breath and sits down at the kitchen table, tapping the seat next to her for me to do the same. I count to five before sitting down.

"I'm sorry, Rosi. I'm worried about you. We all know that Wesley is dating again. I just think it'd be good for your self-confidence if you started dating again, too. You don't want to be alone at your dad's and my age, do you?"

"Wesley isn't dating again," I say through gritted teeth. "He's engaged to his mistress. And I don't need a partner to live a happy life. I'm here to help you and Dad when he has his surgery later this week. I am not here as your pet project." I stand up. "I'm taking an orange and going for a walk around the block." I grab the orange out of the fruit bowl again and storm outside.

The neighborhood in Tucson Valley is busy at 8:00 on a Monday morning. Dog walkers give small waves as I pass by, the mountains at their backs. A stern woman with a tiny white poodle walks down the middle of the sidewalk as if she owns it. I have to step into the rocks to the side. Neither she nor her dog reacts to my presence.

12

A light breeze blows my hair into my face. I should have put it up in a ponytail, but some unwritten rule has me convinced that ponytails are reserved for those still in their youth. The fresh, crisp air feels good, though, as I mini meditate on the here and now, having never given myself time to learn how to meditate properly. How has my life gotten to this point? I wasn't supposed to be here in my late 30s. We should be raising a second child still finishing up his or her high school years, but Wesley had crushed that dream when he'd gone in for a vasectomy when Zak was only two years old. I'd only found out when I got home from my job at the newspaper one day and found him on the couch in the living room with a bag of frozen peas on his crotch.

"Good morning, Miss," says an older gentleman who passes me with a large Golden Retriever.

"Good morning. You have a beautiful dog."

"Well, thank you. Suzi's a sweetie. But she's also a whole lot of trouble." He laughs as he strokes his white beard with his free hand.

"Oh?"

"She gave birth to five rambunctious puppies two months ago. She snuck out of the backyard and found herself a friend which came as quite a surprise when the veterinarian told me her weight gain was due to pregnancy and not because I'd been feeding her one too many table scraps. I sure wasn't prepared for the chaos Suzi has brought to my house."

"Oh, well, that is a unique problem," I say, though I wonder why he didn't get Suzi fixed when she was younger if he didn't want to worry about this possibility.

"You don't happen to want a puppy, do you?" His eyes twinkle as he tugs on Suzi's leash until she sits. "Good girl."

"Me? No, thank you. I'm just visiting my parents for a few weeks. I can't possibly take a puppy."

"If you change your mind, let me know. I'm sure I'll see you around the neighborhood. You're Richard's girl, right?"

I smile. It's been a few years since I've been called anyone's *girl*. "Thank you, Mr….?"

"Bob. My name is Bob Horace."

"Nice to meet you, Bob…and you, too, Suzi. Good luck with the puppies."

After Bob and Suzi have continued on their way, I look at my Apple Watch. Shoot! Mom's company will be arriving soon. I turn around, walk up the slight hill, close my eyes for a quick clearing of the mind, and open the front door. Ready or not, I'm here.

Chapter 3

"Jan, Karen, Paula, Brenda, this is my daughter Rosi." She waves her hand through the air above my chest.

I wonder if I'm supposed to bow or something. "Hello." I raise my hand slightly. "Nice to meet you all. Mom has told me so much about you," I lie.

"We've heard so much about *you*," says the woman named Jan.

Jan with the nephew. Ugh.

"Everyone find a chair," says Mom. "Rosi, you'll be seated at the head of the table."

Great. My throne awaits. I smile sweetly, though, and pull out my chair like a dutiful daughter. Breakfast conversation in Tucson Valley is as scandalous as a late-night bar discussion after shots of whiskey. Gossip City.

"Did you hear about Troy and Salem?" asks Paula. She's a large woman with tight curls pressed up against her head. I notice that as she talks her double chin bobbles. I wonder if she gets her hair set like that on purpose every week at the salon.

"It was all the talk at the gym this morning," says Brenda. "I still don't know what Bob saw in that woman." Her too tight face betrays no emotion, and her fake breasts stand at attention, much too high for a sixty-something-year-old woman. I recognize her as the woman with the small white poodle who refused to move on the sidewalk when I passed by.

"I know!" says Jan. "She's the worst. I went into her bookstore last week, and she was so rude!"

"What were you looking for?" asks Karen so quietly that everyone at the table must strain to hear her.

"Oh, a book about the paleo diet," says Jan dismissively.

Karen skulks into the back of her chair and neatly cuts her sausage and egg casserole which Mom has dished out to everyone.

"I heard that Salem slept with Troy Kettleman in the office at Salem's Stories," says Paula.

"And that Bob walked in on them!" gasps Brenda.

"Tsk, tsk, that's terrible," says Mom. "Would anyone like more fruit?"

I can't believe how stereotypical these women are being, the nosy, gossipy, busy-body types who have nothing better to do than to discuss the break-up of someone else's relationship. I imagine the same thing is going on now back in Springfield. All of the moms of the friends of Zak are twittering on about how my husband of twenty years left me for a younger woman, how she'd spent the day at *my house* where Wes worked from home while I covered local news for the Springfield Gazette, attending mundane meetings at city hall or listening to the police scanner for the petty crimes that happened around town.

"What do you think, Rosi?" my mother interrupts my complicated thoughts.

"Excuse me?" Five sets of eyes stare at me awaiting my response to a question I didn't hear.

"Would you like to join our pickleball game tomorrow?" repeats Brenda.

"Oh, sure. Yeah, that sounds fun," I lie through my teeth.

"Great!" says Mom too enthusiastically as she claps her hands together like a young child who's just been told she can have an extra helping of ice cream.

"Did you know that my nephew won two pickleball singles tournaments in Vermont?" Jan asks. All conversation ceases and awaits my response...*again*.

"That's awesome."

"He's a real catch," says Jan. "He was twenty-eighth in his law school class and runs ten miles every week. Isn't that fantastic? But now he is CEO of his own business." She beams as I stare at her fake blonde hair. It looks orange under the light streaming in from the skylight.

"That's amazing," says my mother.

I turn my head and roll my eyes. There's nothing amazing about being outside of the top ten of your law school class or averaging 1.4 miles a day in a week. Heck, even *I* could do that, and I detest running. "Excuse me, ladies, but may I take your plates to the kitchen?" I stand up and start clearing the table, not waiting for their answers.

After I've scraped the plates and loaded the dishwasher, I quietly open the sliding back door to the patio. I pull over a folding chair from the patio onto the rocks in the backyard so that I am hidden from the view of the cackling ladies inside while I sit in the corner. I inhale the fresh February air and wonder again how I got into this position—in Arizona and in life.

Ten minutes later? Twenty minutes later? I've lost track of time. I hear the sliding door open behind me. I turn to see Dad stumbling toward the chair closest to me. It's nice to have quality time together. "How was golf?" I ask, pointing to his bum knee which he's trying to get as much mileage out of as possible before his surgery at the end of the week.

"Good. I can hold my own. Finished strong with a couple of birdies."

"That's great, Dad. Tucson Valley seems good for you. I'm glad you are enjoying yourself here."

"I am, Rosi. It's a lovely community."

"Uh-huh."

He puts his hand on my arm until I turn to face him. "Mom terrorized you this morning, didn't she?"

I nod my head.

"She's just so dang proud to show you off, Rosi."

I nod again.

"I'm serious, Rosi. She's so excited to have you here."

"She's only glad to help out a friend by trying to hook me up with her nephew." I look past my dad at the cactus wren that is resting on the stone wall between my parents' house and their neighbor's, aside a row of cacti that form a privacy barrier.

"Tell her no."

I raise an eyebrow as I look at my dad, really look at him. He's aged a lot in the past year. Despite trying very hard to remain active, his body has failed him. In addition to his upcoming knee surgery, he's had cataract surgery on his eyes and started varicose vein treatment for his legs. "Have you ever told mom *no*?"

"I have—once," he chuckles. "But seriously, you are a successful, grown woman. Set the boundaries you are comfortable with."

"I don't know about the successful part." I stretch my back, thinking that maybe I'm at the sitting-too-long-causes-back-pain stage.

"You've been with the newspaper for ten years. You have your own weekly column, for goodness' sake. That's successful in my eyes."

"No offense, Dad, but your eyes aren't what they used to be. But thanks for the pep talk. I'd better go in and say goodbye before Mom gets mad at me for ditching the table."

"Too late for that. They left five minutes ago."

Chapter 4

Since Mom is giving me the cold shoulder today after my bailing on her friends "in the most embarrassing display of lack of manners ever," I've decided to get out of the house and explore a bit of Tucson Valley on my own. Dad has left for one more round of golf with his buddies though I still can't fathom how he can complete 18 holes on his stiff knee.

I grab a cloth shopping bag from the front closet, put on my tennis shoes, and leave a note on the fridge. *Going out for a bit. I'll bring back dessert for dinner.* My mea culpa. Mom is watering plants on the back patio when I sneak out the front door.

The sunshine feels amazing. In the Midwest, clouds seem to linger in the winter, making the need for Vitamin D pills essential, at least for me, especially after the year I've lived through. I pull out my phone to check my GPS. There's a little bookstore I've scouted out already along with a bakery about a half mile away in downtown Tucson Valley. Tucson Valley Retirement Community is located on the edge of the city.

I pass Brenda with the white poodle. She doesn't smile—again—until she recognizes me as Renee's daughter.

22

"Rosi?"

"Hello, Brenda. It's nice to see you again." The white poodle bares his teeth. I take a step back.

"Don't mind Ralphie. He senses when people are being untruthful." She stares a second too long.

"Uh, okay. I hope you have a great day," I lie again as I wave and make a wide loop around her and Ralphie into the street.

A landscaping team is planting in a communal area between the stop sign on the next block and the sidewalk. I could get used to seeing blooming flowers this time of year.

"Sorry about the mess, miss," a man yells as he jumps up from the ground to kick dirt off the sidewalk from where a crew of workers had been tilling the dirt for a variety of plants waiting to be put into the ground.

"It's okay," I say, smiling. "The flowers are pretty. What are they?"

The man wipes his hands on his khaki pants. A gentle smile conveys a real love for his job when he talks. "These are sweet William plants," he says, admiring a deep red plant with a pale, pink-colored center. "And the orange flowers are calendula."

"I assume these are plants that do well in a desert?"

"I hope so, but that's why I have a job. My team will make sure that these beauties get plenty to drink." He runs his hand through his thick, dark hair, and even though it's only in the sixties, a bead of sweat slides down his face.

I laugh. "That makes sense. Sorry, I'm not from here. I guess that was a stupid question."

"Nothing stupid about it at all. I love talking about plants, so I'm happy to answer your questions. Where are you from if you don't mind me asking?"

"Sure. I'm visiting my parents for a few weeks. My dad is having knee replacement surgery this week. I'm from Illinois."

"Chicago. That's quite a big city."

I shake my head wildly. "No, no. I'm from central Illinois."

"Sorry!" He puts his hand up. "I didn't mean to offend."

"It's fine. Most people assume that Chicago *is* Illinois. I love Chicago, but I am a small-town girl."

He grins again. "Then you should love it here in Tucson Valley. It's quite small with a mix of some of the fun of a big city, you know," he says, bending closer and whispering, "for the older people."

I grin. "I completely understand. My parents rave about all there is to do here. I'm afraid I'm going to be subjected to many of those *fun* things, too."

"Don't rule them out yet. I think you may find that there is something magical about this place."

I stare at this hard-working, kind man far longer than is comfortable, and I realize he's the first person I've talked to today who didn't view me with contempt. "My name's Rosi," I say, sticking out my hand. "Thanks for the botany lesson today."

"Keaton," he says, wiping his hands yet again on his pant legs before taking my hand in his.

"That's an unusual name."

"I know." He shakes his head back and forth. "My mom was a huge fan of Alex P. Keaton on Family Ties, Michael J. Fox's character. I was born in 1982, the year that show aired."

I don't mean to laugh, but it's what happens.

Keaton drops his head in embarrassment.

I put my hand on Keaton's arm. "I'm sorry. I'm not laughing at you. I love the name. I'm laughing because I'm named after an '80s sitcom, too. I'm Rosisophia Doroche, Rosi, for short."

Keaton's eyes grow large, and he chuckles, a hearty sound that fills the void between us with merriment. "The Golden Girls? Oh, man, that's the best. Thanks for making my day."

I can feel the heat rising up my face.

Keaton sees it, too. "Are you okay?"

I nod my head. "Yes, but…but I've never told anyone in my life what my given name was." I open my eyes wide in horror after I realize what I've done.

"It's okay, Rosi. I think it's cool. *Crazy* cool, maybe. But, hey, I'm a sitcom kid, too. We're all out here living our lives, just trying to find the joy, right? And you sure made my day."

I study the man before me, getting his hands dirty to make the town look nicer for the wealthy snowbirds that live here, escaping to their second homes to frolic in the sunshine and warmth. I wonder if they realize what strangers are doing to add to their experience. "Thanks, Keaton. You've made my day, too." I tuck a strand of hair behind my ear, starting to sweat myself. "Maybe I'll see you around."

"I'd like that," he says. "And my friends call me Keats."

I am still smiling when I get to the Tucson Valley bookstore, Salem's Stories. It was touted online as having *anything you could possibly want* along with specializing in vintage books which includes a pretty lucrative online vintage book business from the looks of things on the website. I'm also excited to meet *the* Salem who caused such a tizzy with Mom and her friends yesterday at brunch when her name came up during their gossip session.

"Oh my!" I call out as I am greeted at the door by a rowdy tan-colored puppy that is jumping on my legs and biting my shoes.

"Barley! Barley! Stop it. Stop it!" A tall woman with enough jewelry that might cause the average woman to tip over, gets up, grabs the collar of the dog, and pulls him off my leg.

"He's a friendly welcoming crew."

"She," is all the woman says as she's dragging Barley back to her desk where she barricades *her* with four other dogs of similar coloring and excitement.

I leave the woman to her tasks, which at this moment seems to be wrangling five rambunctious puppies who are twisting themselves over and around her legs while she has a stack of boxes on her desk that I presume to be

27

new books. To describe the bookstore as crowded is an understatement. The narrow rows of books are full from the bottom shelves that lie just above the avocado-colored carpet to the panels of the dropped ceiling. There are books that sit upon chairs at the end of the aisles and even books stacked upon the floors of some of the more popular sections. I peruse the thriller books while side-stepping the cozy mysteries that sit on the floor, wondering if they get a second look from customers as they literally can't be missed because they block the path of forward movement.

An odd smell permeates throughout the shop, a mix of stale cigarette smoke and expensive perfume. I imagine the avocado carpet could tell quite the story of this place. I jump as I turn the corner into the fiction section when the woman from the front of the store is standing in my path staring at me.

She waves her hands around wildly as if wanting me to survey her inventory with a simple swoop of my eyes. "Finding what you need?" she asks dryly.

"Oh, yes, thank you. I'm just browsing."

She sighs loudly. "That's what they all do nowadays. Can't anyone be drawn to a bookstore anymore for the sincere desire to find that one special book they've been dying to get their hands on?"

I assess the woman. She's draped in a black caftan that flows to the floor, much like her over-dressed bookshelves. Her hair, pulled into a tight bun matches the color of her caftan, and the makeup upon her face looks as if it's been painted on, much too perfect to be real. I assess her as someone who's tried very hard to look younger than her decades though the cracks come through, even with her painted-on makeup. "I do enjoy a good beach read. Do you have any new Elin Hilderbrand or Dorthea Benton Frank books?" I smile. In my job as a newspaper reporter, I've had my share of difficult personalities to interview. I have found that *confusing them with kindness* truly is the best motto though I've altered the statement to read in my mind as *killing them with kindness* as the situation warrants for the particular person I am interviewing.

"Of course, I have those books. Does it look like I wouldn't have bestsellers like that?" She scowls, her unnaturally arched eyebrows falling further down her forehead. "Follow me."

I am amused more than annoyed by the woman's demeaner. I think that expanding upon our conversation might be fun. "How long has Salem's Stories been in Tucson Valley?" I ask after the woman has stopped in front of a stack of beach reads marked with a small handwritten sign that says, *beach reads*. Clear advertising.

"I've been here for thirty years." She assesses me for the first time, running her eyes up and down my body from head to toe. "You're new to Tucson Valley," she says matter-of-factly.

"I am. I'm staying with my parents. My dad is having knee replacement surgery tomorrow."

"Like every other old geezer in this town," she guffaws. "Not everyone takes as good care of themselves as they should." She doesn't smile or take her eyes off me.

"I think the body is a reflection of a life well-lived. And sometimes the effects of a well-lived life show up in a negative way—bad knees and all. Much as people get *face tune-ups*," I say, staring at her taut skin, "they may need knee joint replacements." I'm done confusing this woman with kindness. She's a bit of a shrew.

"Hmph," is all she says before turning around and returning to the front of the bookstore and her yelping puppies.

I pick out two new-to-me beach reads and a map of southern Arizona. There's something rewarding about opening a map to chart your route and then spending five minutes trying to refold it just right. It's way more satisfying than using your fingers to pinch open a map on your iPhone. "I'm ready to check out now."

The woman is entering information on her computer. She looks as if it's the first time she's seen me. The dogs start barking and jumping, their paws scraping the tops of the counter. "Get down. Get down!" she yells and swats the dogs back to the floor though they aren't deterred and jump back up again.

"I do have another question for you," I say, the woman stopping midway through calculating my purchases.

She's put on glasses and peers at me over the top of them. "Yes?"

"Are you Salem—the bookstore's namesake?"

"I am," she says, the first smile I've seen from her, spreading across her face. "The one and only."

"That's lovely. My mom and her friends were telling me about your store. I had to check it out for myself."

"Who is your mother?" Her glasses have slipped to the end of her nose.

"Renee Laruee."

She exhales loudly.

"Is there a problem?" My defense reflex kicks in.

"Renee is fine, but her so-called friends are a bunch of cackling hens. They are nauseating."

I really can't argue with Salem's thoughts, so I don't say anything. Plus, the feeling is mutual from their perspective about Salem.

"Do you want a dog?" she asks unexpectedly.

"Excuse me?"

"My ex-boyfriend won't leave me alone—and that includes dropping these incessant beasts off at my shop every day. I can't keep them. I don't *want* to keep them."

"They are adorable, but I'm here for only a few weeks."

"That's what they all say," she mumbles under her breath.

"And I don't think my parents want a puppy in their house while Dad is recuperating from surgery."

"Dogs are the best medicine, right? Don't they say something like that?" She rolls her eyes as she pushes another dog head back down below the counter in a whack-a-mole effort.

Just then the chime on the front door rings. We both turn toward the door. The gentleman who'd been walking his Golden Retriever yesterday walks in. A bell goes off in my head. Bob? Was that his name? Bob's dog is the parent of these puppies. *Bob—sweet Bob—*is Salem's ex. I shudder involuntarily.

"Thank heavens! Take these foolish rats out of my store. They are destroying my civility."

"Hello, Salem. Rosi?" He looks at me with a large smile of recognition on his face.

"You know him?" she asks me in surprise.

"Of course she knows me, Salemite. I'm a popular guy with *most* of Tucson Valley, if only you'd see that," he sighs.

"Don't call me that!" she barks, almost as loud as the puppies who are howling for the treats that Bob is throwing on the floor behind the counter.

"Did you find some treasures, Rosi?" Bob asks, the smile not leaving his face.

"I did. Thanks. Are these Suzi's puppies?"

"Aren't they beauties?" he asks. "Say, have you changed your mind about the puppies now that you've seen

33

how adorable they are? Would you like to purchase one of them? I'll make you a deal—the pretty girl special."

Salem snorts from her chair where she has returned to entering numbers into her computer despite the fact that she hasn't given me my final total yet. "I tried to *give* away your mongrels. You think she'd *pay* for one?"

"I am flattered that you'd ask, Bob, but I don't think that this is the right time in my life for a dog."

"There is never a bad time for the *right dog*, Rosi. Think about it. Until then, I need to take these beauties back to their Mama. Thanks for babysitting, Salem." She ignores him while he leashes them up, one by one, and walks out of the store.

Salem doesn't say a word as she finishes my transaction. I wonder what Bob ever saw in Salem to have given her the opportunity to make him her ex. She puts a card inside my bag that says *Salem's Stories Vintage Finds—Online Auction Sales*. I take my books and flee from the craziest book shopping experience of my life.

Chapter 5

"What did you do today, Rosi?" Dad asks as he scoops a large helping of mashed potatoes out of a bowl, part of his last meal before he begins his fast for his knee replacement surgery tomorrow.

"Well, I met a landscaper who taught me about sweet William and calendula flowers."

"You met Keaton, I imagine," says Mom, breaking her silent treatment after being *so angry she could cry* (her words) since I'd gone outside instead of staying to visit with her friends until the bitter end.

"Yes, that was his name." Mom is unusually quiet. I take the bait. "Do you have a problem with him?" I ask. "Has he killed some of your prized plants with his landscaping techniques?" I hide my smile behind a basket of rolls that Dad passes to me.

"No, of course not. He's a fine landscaper, one of the best in the retirement community." She takes a long sip of her wine.

"Then what's the matter?"

"Nothing is the matter."

Dad and I both give her a knowing look.

"Well, fine then. Keaton is the son of illegal immigrants. There, I've said it."

"And how do you know this bit of news, Renee?"

"He told Brice Holland who told his mother who told Brenda who told Paula who told me that they were deported a year ago, though Keaton was born in the States, of course."

Dad slams down his glass of water so hard that some spills over the top. "That settles it then. Keaton, the landscaper, is a terrible person because he was born in the United States to parents who never pursued the path to citizenship but wanted to give him a better life. Shame, shame, shame," he shakes his head in a sarcastic attempt at disappointment.

"You're not being funny, Richard."

"Mom, you really need to stop with the gossip. From what I saw today, Keaton is just doing his part to make Tucson Valley look pretty for all of you. Nothing in his backstory should sour your judgments. Without his parents—who may well be fine people—you wouldn't have Keaton tending to the beautification of your community."

Mom smiles, though I know it's disingenuous. "You're right. Eat up before your food gets cold."

"What time do you need to be at the hospital tomorrow, Dad?"

"Seven o'clock, but your mom will take me. You sleep in. We will need your help more after I'm home."

"Are you sure?" I look between my parents who are both nodding their heads in agreement.

"Okay. I'll tidy up and read my new books that I bought today until you get home from the procedure. Let me get that chocolate pie I bought." I get up from the table.

"Did you meet Salem today?" asks Mom when I come back from the kitchen with a glorious pie covered with a thick whipped cream topping.

"I did. She's...unique?" I wrinkle my nose at the memory of the rude woman with the overzealous puppies.

"She's a witch," says my conservative mother, her closest attempt at swearing. "Not a *witch* witch, but you know...a witch. Well, she might *be* a *witch* witch, too, since her name is Salem, after all."

I laugh. "I get it, Mom. She won't receive any invites from the Tucson Valley Senior Club."

"Absolutely not."

"What I think your mother is trying to say," says Dad as he leans in as if he's preparing to tell a secret though it is only the three of us at the dinner table. "She likes to make herself *available,* shall I say, to the Tucson Valley men, and most of the women attached to those men frown upon the offer."

"Today she was puppy sitting for that nice man I met when I was walking yesterday; Bob's his name."

Mom makes an audible sound of disgust, a contortion of sounds emanating from her throat. "Bob is a foolish man."

"Bob is a kind man," Dad corrects. "But he has poor taste in women. He's been divorced three times."

"Love the gossip, but I'm going to take another walk and then settle in for the evening. Mom, leave the dishes, and I'll take care of them when I get back."

Mom nods her head in agreement. She's more concerned about Dad's surgery than she's been letting on. Dad is her rock, and even something as benign as a knee replacement surgery has her on edge.

Tonight I head south when I leave my parents' house. It's new territory for me though all of the homes look identical: brown stucco with black lampposts in front of each home, arch-shaped carports allowing for a single car. It'd be easy to get lost. I pull out my phone to look at the GPS map of the area. My new Southwest Arizona map doesn't have the neighborhood details I need tonight. I have a new text I'd missed as even as an adult I'd abided by my mother's no phone at the table rule and put it on *do not disturb*. I stare at the name on my phone. *Wesley*. I open the message.

Need to discuss the house. Don't ignore this message.

I close my eyes and take a deep breath, counting to ten. It's something my therapist taught me to do when Wes upsets me, as he's the only one who can push my buttons to a point of rage. When Grandma Kate died, she'd left her house to me. My parents were aghast that an eighteen-year-old would be given a house. Simon had been given her car—a 1987 Buick—and he was only fourteen. The house was small, a cute two bedroom, one-and-a-half bath home in a transitional neighborhood that would only continue to transition until it became *the* most popular neighborhood in Springfield. When Wesley and I met at the state capital where we were both interning for Representative Smithy during college, we'd whirlwind dated, married, and decided to live in my house. We were so young, trying to finish college and start a family at the same time. I added his name to the deed; we added a bedroom and a bathroom, and the value of the house grew by 300 percent. Now he wants half of the sale of our home. And I don't agree. We'd delayed the finalization of our divorce for months trying to find a common ground on the issue, but in the end, we'd signed the divorce papers while still sharing the responsibility for a home equity loan in both our names since we'd started a huge renovation project two years before our marriage fell apart. Now there is nothing about the updates I can enjoy. It only makes me sad to see the pretty soapstone countertops in the kitchen when I'm having my coffee. What could have been will never be.

"Stop it! Quit biting! Stop biting my leg!"

The noises come from behind me. I turn around to see a boy, maybe a teenager, who is trying to manage what looks like the same puppies I'd seen in Salem's Stories earlier today. "Can I help you?" I ask.

The boy looks up from the pack of dogs and nods his head. I can barely make out his eyes which are covered by bangs that hide half of his face. "If you have any suggestions on how to manage these beasts, I'd take your help."

I take two of the leashes, untangling them from each other, and put one in each hand, a puppy along each side. That allows the boy the chance to untangle his dogs, two leashes in one hand and one in the other. "Are these Bob's puppies?"

He looks up in surprise. "Do you know Grandpa?"

"Well, not really. I met him when he was walking an adult Golden, and today I saw the puppies with Salem when I was shopping in her store when he came to pick them up."

"The puppies were her idea. Everything was always Salem's idea. Then she cheated on my grandpa and left him with this mess." He gestures toward the puppies who have now tired themselves out and are lying on the sidewalk.

"They sure are a cute problem to have," I say, wondering if Bob's account of Suzi getting out of the yard is the real story of Suzi's problem children.

"I guess." A slight smile spreads across his face. There is definitely a resemblance to his grandfather when his dimples come out.

"Do you live with your grandpa?"

"No. I'm visiting. My parents are traveling in Europe."

"Oh! That's quite an adventure."

"Yeah, if you like old, broken-down buildings and too many people gawking at the same things."

I laugh. He reminds me of Zak, as I imagine Zak didn't much like spending time with Wesley and me during the last couple years of our marriage. "I'd be happy to get these puppies back home if you don't mind me walking with you."

"Really? That'd be great. The house is just up the block and around the corner. You've got Barley and Wheatie," he says, pointing to the tired-out pups who are resting peacefully at my feet.

"Come on, Barley. Come, Wheatie." The dogs raise their ears at the sounds of their names but don't budge.

"Let's get a treat!" yells the boy.

That works. All of the puppies jump up and begin running ahead of us, anticipating a reward. I have to jog to keep up with Barley and Wheatie.

Bob meets us in his driveway when we get to his stucco-sided home, identical to my parent's house. "I was just about to look for you. I was concerned that you got lost. Hi, Rosi. What are you doing here?" He grins at me as he reaches down to pet all of the puppies, pulling dog treats from his pocket and delivering them to the eager pups.

"I saw…uh, your grandson, and he looked like he could use some help."

"Yes, sending Devin out with all of the puppies at once was probably not a good idea. Thanks for helping."

"No problem." Something odd catches my attention from inside his open garage. "What do you have in there?" I ask, pointing to several plastic containers that are lined up on a long table in the garage.

"Homemade beer! Would you like a taste?" His smile grows animatedly.

"No, thanks," I laugh. "It's a little late for that," I say as the sun is setting behind the mountains. "Are the containers plastic?"

"They sure are! I'm experimenting, but I've had good luck with plastic bottles."

"Cool. My husband…my ex-husband used to brew beer in our basement." Speaking the truth about my marriage out loud makes me sad. "I need to get back to my parents. See you around, Bob. And Devin."

"Thanks again, Rosi!"

As I walk back to my parents, I wonder again what such a nice guy like Bob could have seen in someone like Salem of Salem's Stories, although who am I to judge her for making poor relationship choices?

Chapter 6

I drive into town today to purchase plants for the front of my parents' house. Inspired by my conversation with Keaton yesterday, I think a yard facelift might put a smile on my parents' faces when they return from the hospital. I park in front of the garden center. I'm not accustomed to the purchase of blooming outside plants in February. In the Midwest, we are cautioned against buying new plants until after Mother's Day.

After picking out geraniums, snapdragons, and petunias—assured by the salesclerk that they are perfect winter Arizona annuals—I check the time. My parents will be home in two hours, plenty of time to get the plants in the pots I've also purchased. Feeling accomplished, I glance down Main Street. I decide to treat myself to a frappe at the coffee shop I noticed yesterday next to the bookstore. I put my plants into the car and walk into the coffee shop.

"Where's Salem?" asks an older woman with a gray ponytail wagging back and forth in the air as she speaks to another woman in hot pink yoga pants.

"I have no idea, Netty. Salem's usually the first shop open on Main Street. Maybe she's at the post office mailing off some of those rare books she sells."

"Maybe," says ponytail lady. "I need to get Jen Moraney's new book before my trip to Mexico. I'm running out of time."

"Check back later. You'll get your book, honey. Don't you worry about a thing," says yoga pants lady.

After receiving my frappe, I walk toward Salem's Stories, motivated by the coffee shop conversation. It does seem odd that a storeowner would walk out of her store during business hours. Plus, I'm wondering if she's puppy sitting again.

The door chimes as I enter Salem's Stories. The lights are all on. The puppies are there again, excited by my entry. I reach over the counter and pet them all. Barley licks my fingers. The puppies have knocked over their water bowl, a pool of water creeping toward a mess of computer cords under Salem's desk. Salem's computer screen has gone dark, and her cellphone is on the desk next to it. "Hello?" I call. No answer. I grab a fistful of tissues from the box on the counter, climb over the puppy gate, and wipe up the water before it reaches the cords. I squat down and let the puppies share their love which puts a smile on my face.

I step back over the gate. "Hello?" I call out again. Curious, I walk down the self-help aisle. Books like *Find Your Feelings* and *Turn Inside Out* stare at me. "Hello? Salem?"

I pass by a wooden train table in the children's book section. All of the train cars are lined up side by side in a perfect row awaiting an engineer. Passing a door marked as *Bathroom,* I walk toward the fiction books. I turn the corner by the mystery books when I stop short. Lying in the middle of the floor in front of the Mysteries A-M sign is a body—the body of Salem.

My hand is shaking as I pull out my phone to call 911. I do as they instruct and check for a pulse. There is none. I can't look away from the body, wishing the police would get here. I've seen dead bodies before in Springfield while covering stories for the paper, but usually it's after the fact when the press gets a tip about an accident or a murder. I've never been the first person on the scene with a body that's not yet cold. A small amount of blood oozes from Salem's head where she's possibly made contact with a metal chair that sits at the end of the aisle, holding a stack of Stephen King novels. The irony is not lost on me. More books litter the floor near her feet, while a pool of liquid sits in a puddle near the body, though I can't tell from where it comes. One thing that is true of all the dead bodies I've seen: They'd all had such different plans when their day started. What a sad state of affairs.

"Bark! Bark! Bark!"

A puppy comes barreling past the row of books, jumping over Salem's body to reach me.

"Barley! What are you doing out?" I grab the dog by the collar and hold her close to me while awaiting the police, hoping she is a super jumper, and I didn't loosen the gate enough that four other puppies will be joining us any minute. Barley sits still next to my leg, recognizing the seriousness of the situation.

The front door chimes. "I'm back here!" I yell, hoping it's not the woman from the coffee shop wanting her romantic comedy for her trip to Mexico.

A pair of paramedics and two police officers appear. The paramedics check for a pulse and confirm my analysis. Salem is dead, definitely dead.

"Don't touch anything else," says the male police officer, a tiny man with large hands and a large nose. What a strange looking creature.

The female officer is a tall woman though anyone would look tall next to the male officer. She has pretty features with large blue eyes and an easy smile. She pulls out a camera and starts taking pictures.

The male officer turns to me. "Hello. Are you the one who called in this scene?" he asks, casually passing his hand over Salem's body, as if there is anyone else in the store who could possibly make that phone call.

"I am," I say both annoyed and curious.

"And who are you?"

He looks me up and down as if I'm applying for a runway model job. Though those days of side hustle modeling for local retail shops are long gone, I'm put together enough to hold myself, at 39, up against any 35-year-old in a competition for looks. I know that and I own that, but being ogled by the retirement community police officer is unsettling. "I'm Rosi Laruee. My parents own a house in town, and I'm visiting for a few weeks."

"Okay," he says slowly. "And why were you in Salem's Stories today?"

"Well, I shopped here yesterday, and I wanted to come back and…and see the puppies." I point to Barley who I am still holding at bay from disturbing the scene. I leave out the part about overhearing the odd conversation at the coffee shop.

"And how did you discover Ms. Mansfield?"

"Well, I discovered her dead, Officer…?"

"Officer Daniel…Officer Dan Daniel," he says, puffing out his chest as if that helps his credibility.

"Officer Daniel, I called as soon as I discovered the body."

"Did you touch anything?" he asks.

"Only her neck where I checked for a pulse under the direction of the 911 dispatcher. Then I stepped back and held onto Barley."

"Barley?" He wrinkles his brow.

"Barley is the dog. She was loose, unlike the other puppies who were behind the counter by the front door.

"Did you let her loose?"

"Of course not. Why would I do something like that?"

"Well, Ms. Laruee, we will need to take your fingerprints at the station later today, so please…"

"*My fingerprints?* Why on earth do you need to take my fingerprints?" I'm so flustered I let go of Barley, and she jumps on Officer Daniel, licking his giant nose.

"Take this hairy beast. I need to call animal control."

"Wait! Don't do that. I know the owner. Well, I kind of know him and where he lives. I'll get the dogs to him. Don't call animal control."

Officer Daniel assesses me again before shaking his head in agreement. "Fine. You can take the dogs, but I need those fingerprints."

"I don't understand. Are you accusing me of something? Has Salem been murdered?"

"Mrs. La…"

"Ms."

"Ms. Larue, there is blood at the scene. That indicates foul play."

"That could also mean that she hit her head when she fell."

"And why would she have fallen?"

"I don't know! I was just shopping! How would I know? But this place is kind of a mess!" I am yelling now.

The female officer steps away from the body. "Ms. Laruee, we need your prints just so we can compare them against any others that might be on the body. If there are others, we will focus on those, of course. There is no reason to presume you were doing anything here but shopping, as you said." She smiles, her perfectly aligned teeth shining. "I'm Officer Kelly."

"Kelly Kelly?" I ask before I can stop myself.

"No, Morgan Kelly," she chuckles. Officer Dan Daniel shoots her a dirty look. "Give us your contact information, and you can be on your way. Thank you for your time. And thank you for taking the dogs."

"Yes, of course."

"Why don't you come by the station tomorrow? You are a bit busy today," she says, stopping to pet Barley who wags her tail. "Right, Officer Daniel?"

"Fine. But make it early. We don't have many suspicious deaths in Tucson Valley. This is an important case."

A chiming clock surprises us all. Eleven chimes. I hear them all. "Oh, no! I have to go. My dad's getting home from surgery!" I don't wait for an answer as I throw my old business card from the *Springfield Gazette* at Officer Daniel and run to the front of the store. Barley follows. I find the puppies' leashes easily, grab a bag of food that is in a plastic container, and scurry out the door with five new friends before I can logically change my mind.

Chapter 7

I pull into the driveway of my parents' house mere seconds before my parents pull in behind me with Karen's car. She'd been so kind as to lend them her car this morning so that I could have a car to run errands with. This is not how I'd planned the day: plant some pretty new flowers, run the vacuum, cook a nice lunch. Now, instead, I've done none of those things, *and* I've come home with five very frisky puppies. How am I going to be able to explain this?

I crack open the windows, knowing that the comfortable temperature is safe for a five-minute stint in the car while I try to figure this out. "Hey Mom, Dad. How are you?" I open Dad's door and hand him the walker I'd set outside the front door this morning before I went to town.

"A bit sore, Rosisophia Doroche, but only going up from here." He raises himself with the walker and walks toward the garage, shuffling his feet as he walks.

I try to keep my body between him and the car so he doesn't notice the dogs until I can figure out what I am going to do with them, but they aren't cooperating. The barking is deafening.

"What on Earth?" asks Mom as she peers inside their car, the poor leather interior likely being scratched. "Rosi?" Mom turns to me as her eyes grow larger by the second.

"I promise I can explain. I'm not keeping them, Mom. You have to trust me. We only need to keep them here until I can find Bob, the owner. I can't keep them in your car, though. It's not super hot, but they're puppies, and puppies, well, you know. Puppies need to run around. Puppies need to pee *outside*. So, I need to ask you a huge favor. I need to keep the dogs tied up in the backyard. I'll put them in the rocks, not on the patio. They may be here an hour or two tops." I stop talking and look at my mother who is petting Barley through the top of the opened window. I'm shocked. I've never known my mother to pay any attention to a four-legged creature.

"They can stay on the patio. It's too sunny to be in the rocks. You can hose the potty when they're gone."

She follows Dad who has already gone into the house, likely seeking out his recliner. I'm pleased with her reaction but also surprised. I hope I don't owe her for this favor. Aren't *I* the one doing Bob a favor by keeping his puppies away from animal control?

I drag the dogs around the side of the house, letting us in through the gate to the backyard. I unleash the dogs who immediately begin scurrying around the backyard marking their territory. Once I know they are settled with food and water from the hose in an empty bucket I'd found near Dad's gardening supplies, I open the sliding door into the house.

"I've got lunch!" I yell into the living room. "I'll bring sandwiches right out." Thank goodness Mom went shopping yesterday as I've totally failed in my whole purpose of being here to help my parents.

"You might be wondering about the dogs," I say after Mom and Dad have received their sandwiches.

"I guess you could say we're a bit curious as to why there is a dog sleeping on my lounge chair and another humping my bird feeder."

"Oh no," I say, looking out the slider at Wheatie who is doing just as described. I sigh. "When I went into town today—to get new plants to surprise you with—I went back to the bookstore. I found Salem Mansfield, the owner."

"What do you mean you *found her*?" asks Mom, who is only picking at her sandwich, still too worried about Dad to focus on eating.

"She was dead."

"What?" she yells as she throws her sandwich back on her plate.

"She was lying on the ground."

"What happened?" Dad asks, sitting up in his chair and wiping crumbs off his face.

"I have no idea, but she'd been watching Bob's puppies. I guess they used to date as I've heard, and…"

"Bob Horace. Those are Bob Horace's dogs?" asks Mom.

"Yes. He lives a couple of blocks over. I've run into him with his large Golden Retriever, the puppies' mother. He'd also been to the shop yesterday when I bought some new books. He was picking up the puppies. The puppies were there again today. I told the police I'd get them to the owner. They were going to call animal control. I couldn't let that happen."

"That's understandable, Rosi," says Dad who makes a wincing face.

"Dad, do you need your pain medicine?" I ask, reaching for a prescription bottle.

"No, not that. I'll take some ibuprofen, though. The bottle's over there," he says, pointing to the coffee table. "That's all I need."

"Dead," Mom says quietly. "I can't believe that Salem is dead. I mean, I'm not *sad*. Is that bad that I'm not sad?" She doesn't wait for an answer. "I'm just surprised. So many people hated that woman. I wonder if someone killed her. Or was it an accident? Or a medical emergency?" she asks, as questions swirl around in her mind. "Did you see blood, Rosi?"

"Only from where she hit her head when she fell. Don't start spreading rumors now, Mom. Let the police do their job, although from my observation of the lead officer that I met today, this might be a bumbling investigation. They want *my* fingerprints! Can you believe that?"

"Whatever for?" asks Mom.

"Something about needing to rule out my fingerprints with any others that might be on the body. I checked for her pulse and called 911."

"Oh my. That must have been terrible," says Mom. "Was she…how did she…uh, look?"

"What a horrid question, Renee," says Dad, shaking his head.

"She looked dead, Mom, not murdered. There was a little bit of blood around her head and a puddle of something wet around her legs."

"Did she slip on something?"

"Renee? Stop with the speculation," says Dad.

"What? Rosi doesn't want me to gossip. It's not gossiping if I have *facts* to share."

"I'm not sure that's how gossip works, Mom. Dad, can I get you anything before I return the dogs to Bob?"

"Thanks, Rosi. Hand me my remote control over there," he says, pointing to the coffee table where the remote sits next to a Betty White bobblehead.

I hand Dad his remote control and a cookie from the jar Mom had stocked yesterday. I think that maybe they don't really need my help and just wanted company. "Do you have a number for Bob?" I ask Mom who is sitting as close to Dad as humanly possible without being on his lap. She's going to suffocate him with her concern.

"Let me call Jan. She knows everybody."

A few minutes later, Mom returns with a piece of paper and a phone number. "Here you go. Jan said she heard from Brenda who heard from Karen that Salem was missing this morning when Netty went in for a travel book on Nantucket which means she may have been dead for a long time. I still can't believe that she's been killed."

"Nobody said that Salem's been killed, Mom. She died. She could just have easily died from a heart attack." And I don't mention that *Netty* with the gray ponytail wasn't looking for a travel book to Nantucket but a beach read for her trip to Mexico. What would they do with that bit of information? "Thanks for the number," I say, plucking the paper from her hand before I have to listen to any more of her theories.

Bob and his grandson meet me on the driveway of my parents' house twenty minutes later.

"Rosi, you are a lifesaver. I just can't believe any of this. First, my dear, sweet Salem has died, and then my puppies have disappeared. I can't imagine why any of this has happened. No one would hurt that poor woman." He blinks rapidly, wiping his eyes with the back of his hand.

Devin rolls his eyes behind his grandpa. *"She was crazy,"* he whispers to me.

I am not about to get in the middle of this disagreement. "I am very sorry for your loss. I am sure it's quite a shock. But I do have the puppies, and they are completely safe. Come see them for yourselves." The puppies smother Bob and Devin with attention when they walk in the backyard, jumping all over them. Only Barley jumps on me.

"I think she's partial to you, Rosi. You should keep her." Bob gestures toward Barley who is licking my toes and the tops of my sandals.

"I can't keep her, Bob."

"Yes, yes, that's what you are going to do. It's my thanks to you for rescuing the puppies from animal control and for finding my sweet Salem."

"No, I really can't…"

"Yes, Rosi. I think you should keep her."

I turn around to see my mother who is sitting on a patio chair. "Mom?"

"Yes, Rosi. You need company. That dog will be good company when Zak's with Wesley or at school. Plus, she'll be good security, too. Take her."

"It really is rude to argue with your mother," Bob says.

Barley rubs her head against my leg. I pet the top of her head. She licks my hand.

"What about Dad? He's barely mobile. Having a puppy is not a good idea."

"She can stay in the yard or be on a leash in the house. We will make it work. Keep her, Rosi."

"I think this matter is settled," says Bob. "Thanks again. Salem would be pleased to know someone so kind was going to raise one of her beloved puppies."

Even though his sentiment is sweet, Salem didn't at all seem enamored of the puppies when I shopped yesterday. "Thanks, Bob, and I'm really sorry—again—for Salem's passing."

After Bob has gone, I sit on the ground to pet Barley. She crawls into my lap and puts her head on my knee. I look toward the chair where Mom had been sitting, but she has gone back inside. In front of her chair on the table is an ashtray. I haven't known my mother to smoke for thirty years. What an odd day.

Chapter 8

Call me today or I'm contacting my lawyer.

I slide my phone back into my purse and ignore Wesley's message *again.* I don't want to argue, not from Arizona at least. I'd given him my offer. Grandma Kate left *me* that house years ago, not Wesley and me. We'd lived together in the house for twenty years. It's probably petty, but I put sweat equity into making that house a home to raise our family in, and Grandma Kate never liked Wesley anyway. When he'd turned his nose up at her special hamburger and baked beans casserole the first Fourth of July he'd spent with our family, she'd pulled me aside and said, *Rosi, you can't trust a man who won't eat good old American baked beans.* If only I'd listened to that wise woman way back then, I'd have saved myself a lot of heartache. Splitting the house halfsies is not something I will consider *ever.* I believe that a sixty/forty split of the house sale is fair, especially since we earned nearly the same salaries to contribute to the home equity loan.

The morning had been quiet. I'd sent Mom to water aerobics with her friends because she was driving Dad and me crazy with her hovering. I'd made sure the freezer was full of icepacks for Dad's knee and helped to rearrange furniture so that his knee could be elevated. When she returned home an hour later, I told her there were sandwiches and fruit ready to go in the fridge and that I'd be back after getting fingerprinted at the police station. That is where I am now, ignoring Wesley's text and waiting to be fingerprinted by Officer Dan Daniel.

"Ms. Laruee?" asks Officer Daniel who stands outside his office looking around as if there is a crowd of people in the waiting room though I am the only one here.

"Hello. I'm right here." I raise my hand in the air, realizing that I really need a manicure.

"Right. Please come back to the processing room, and we will get you fingerprinted." A secretary eyes me suspiciously. Why am I being treated like a suspect?

While Officer Daniel is rolling my fingers in the black ink, I make small talk because that's what Midwesterners do, especially if they are reporters. "Any idea what happened to Salem?"

Officer Daniel raises his eyebrows. "Why are you asking?"

So, Officer Daniel is *this* kind of guy. I can play the game, though. "You are clearly taking your job seriously, so I assume you are following every lead. I'm a bit of an amateur detective with the nature of my job, so I could learn from a professional." Stroke his ego, Rosi. Slow and steady.

"Oh, well, yes, of course I am a professional." He straightens his shoulders. "We have working theories, but we are awaiting the toxicology report first. And the lab needs to process any evidence that may have been on Ms. Mansfield's body."

"Like fingerprints?" I ask.

"Yes, exactly—like fingerprints."

"Mr. Horace says he can't imagine anyone wanting to harm Salem," I say as I continue to bait the hook for information. "Do you think that this could all be explained away as an accident?"

Officer Daniel looks to his left and right, leaning close enough that I can feel his warm breath on my face. "Officer Kelly and I think that Salem's death wasn't an accident."

I raise my eyebrows in surprise. "Wow!" I whisper back. "That's terrible. Why do you think that might be…?"

"Hello, Rosi."

I turn around to see Officer Kelly standing behind me. She is smiling. I wonder if she knew that Officer Daniel was spilling secrets.

"Hello, Officer Kelly. Just getting fingerprinted," I say, raising my fingers to show off the black ink.

"Awesome. But remember," she says, putting her hand on my arm. "It's only a precaution—nothing to worry about."

"Of course."

"Did you reunite the puppies with Bob?" asks Officer Daniel.

"I did, well, except for one."

"Did you get conned into keeping a puppy?" asks Officer Kelly. Her bright smile lights up an otherwise drab and dreary room.

"I did—Barley—the one who was with me while I waited for you yesterday.

"Ah, yes. She was a cutie. She's a lucky dog, Rosi," says Officer Daniel.

He touches the same arm that Officer Kelly had just touched, but she didn't make me squirm the same way his touch does. His eyes give off major creepy guy vibes. I am thinking that no amount of information seeking about

Salem's death is worth it if I have to spend any more time with Officer Daniel. "Am I free to go?"

"Of course," says Officer Kelly.

She hands me a wet wipe for my fingers. I turn to leave when someone yells across the room. "Got the toxicology report! Abnormalities! Possibly poison!"

Officer Daniel and Officer Kelly look from each other to me. "Thanks," I say. "Good luck with that."

I turn onto Main Street on my way back to my parents' house when I get a text from my mom. I push the text reader button on the dashboard screen. I love that I can pair my phone with my parents' Honda.

Message from Mom. Shall I read it?

Yes, I say.

Jan and Karen are playing pickleball at 3:00 at the courts in Tuttle Park. Jan thinks you should play so you are ready for next week's game with her nephew.

Do you want to reply? asks the car. What an odd world we live in when we can tell our car to ignore our mother especially since it's my parents' own car I am using.

No, I say definitively.

I pull over to the side of the road to calm myself because I don't want to have this conversation with my mom in person. My mother is going to be the death of me. I just know it.

A knock on my window startles me out of my pity party. I look up and see the soft brown eyes I'd met a couple of days ago. They belong to Keaton, the landscaper. I let my window down.

"Rosi?" He seems surprised, and I'm amazed he remembers my name.

"Hi, Keaton. What are you doing here?"

"I was working on the plant beds in the median," he says, indicating the large planters filled with beautiful purple flowers. "I saw your car stop after you, uh, after you ran the stop sign."

"Oops! I'm a bit distracted."

"Are you okay?" he asks, concern written on his face in a row of tiny wrinkles on his forehead.

"I'm great. Why?" I ask, too chipper for my real mood.

"Well, uh," he hesitates. "Because you have quite a shiner."

He points his finger at my face. I pull down my visor to look in the mirror. Sure enough, there is a giant black smudge under my left eye. I guess I'd done a poor job cleaning my fingers at the police station. I smile. "It's okay. I was just getting my fingerprints taken for Salem's murder."

Keaton takes a step away from my window. "Um, okay. Have a good day then."

"Wait!" I start laughing. I laugh so hard I wonder if I can control the morning's coffee that still sits in my bladder. "Let me explain."

"As long as you don't try to murder me, I'd love to hear your story. I've got thirty minutes for lunch coming up if you want to join me. I have an extra sandwich. But you'll need to move your car. Park up the street, and we can eat at the park down the block."

I am finished wiping all of the black ink off my face when Keaton gets to my car. He waits for me to join him on the sidewalk. I am wondering why I am agreeing to eat lunch with a nearly perfect stranger, yes, a nearly *perfect* stranger. I can't help but notice how well his work khakis hug his assets. It's been a long time since I've noticed such a thing. Has my marriage dulled *everything* in my life including my ability to appreciate the beauty of a hard-working man?

Keaton smiles as we fall into step toward the park. "You really concerned me back there. I thought you'd been in a fight."

"Eek. No, nothing like that. Do you see that kind of thing a lot around Tucson Valley?"

"Of course not. It's a very safe community."

"Then do you have any idea why someone may have killed Salem Mansfield, the owner of Salem's Stories?"

He shakes his head. "No idea. I heard she had died. I didn't know it was murder."

"Well, don't quote me on that. I've just come from the police station, and I heard some rumblings."

Keaton raises an eyebrow and looks at me as we stop at the park entrance. "And did you hear any rumblings about *your* involvement in this said murder?"

"Ah, yes. I still have to explain, don't I?" I take the ham and cheese sandwich that Keaton hands me. We sit at a picnic table that overlooks a dry creek bed, a common view in a desert town.

"Do you make it a habit to find dead bodies?" Keaton asks after I finish telling him about my discovery of

Salem as well as some of the stories I've covered in Springfield.

I can't help but smile. "No. Those are not my favorite stories to cover, but it's part of the job, and someone has to tell those stories, too."

Keaton nods his head. "I suppose. That's why I love being a landscaper—just me and my plants." He laughs, a deep hearty sound that causes a pair of grandmothers with their grandchildren to stare at him.

"Maybe I should consider a career change," I say, sighing. "It sure seems a lot less stressful."

"Unless you tick off the wrong HOA member because they hold strong opinions about foliage—*strong opinions.*"

"I've met a few of those women at my parents' house. Speaking of, I really need to get back. It seems my mother has plans for me this afternoon."

"It was really nice chatting with you, Rosi," says Keaton, as he stands up and zips his lunch bag.

"Yeah, it was nice…I mean…it was nice talking to you, too, Keaton. And thanks for the sandwich!"

"Keats," he says. "Remember my friends call me Keats. I've got a project on the other side of the park. My truck's over there, too, so I'd better get going."

"Maybe I'll see you around."

"I'd like that." He lingers a bit too long as his eyes settle on mine.

"Goodbye, Keats." I know he watches me as I walk back to the car. And I'm thanking the fashion gods that I'd put on white underwear with my light-colored shorts this morning.

I am still smiling when I walk into my parents' house. After checking on Dad and getting him a fresh ice pack for his knee, I walk to the backyard where Mom is hiding in the corner of the patio again. She grabs the ashtray and attempts to hide it under the table when Barley barrels toward me. "Hey, girl. It's nice to see you, too." I let her lick my hands and scratch behind her ears and on her belly as she rolls around on the ground.

"I'm glad you kept her," Mom says, announcing her presence as if I hadn't seen her sitting there the whole time.

I turn around. "Hi, Mom. She's easy to love." Barley flops on top of my feet, so I sit on the ground next to her.

"Do you think I'm easy to love, Rosi?" she asks.

"Mom! What kind of a question is that?"

She purses her lips together and closes her eyes. "I've done a bad thing, Rosi." She hangs her head and inhales slowly.

"Is that why you've been smoking?" I ask, pointing under the table where she is still holding the ashtray.

Her eyes get large, but she doesn't continue the ruse. She sets the ashtray on the table. "It helps my stress, but don't tell Dad. He'd be so disappointed."

"I won't tell Dad—if you don't make me play pickleball today."

"Deal," she says. "Sorry. I just want you to be happy."

"I'm working on it, Mom. The ink on my divorce settlement is barely dry. Give me some time. Okay?"

"Okay."

"Now, what did you do that you think is so bad?"

Mom looks from side to side as if to make sure that no one has materialized in our backyard that will spread her confession. "I accepted a bribe from Salem," she says so quietly I have to lean forward to hear her.

"What do you mean?" Barley rolls over. I scratch her belly again.

"She was counterfeiting books to make them look old and selling them online. She was making a fortune."

"Wow! How do you know this?"

"Because I helped her…once."

Chapter 9

Dad had been thrilled to have an excuse to not attend Salem's funeral today, and I'd been cursed to have to go in his place as Mom's escort. Are funerals the new weddings where everyone gets a plus one? Mom has been on the phone with her gossip group all morning talking about what to wear and what qualifies as too much makeup. I'd left the house after the third call, partly to avoid the silly talk. Salem is dead. Why would she care whether you were wearing eye shadow or not? Plus, none of the women even liked her. The other reason I'd left was to find something more appropriate than the casual shorts and pants I'd packed for my stay to wear to the service. And while Salem certainly won't care what I am wearing, my mother will. And I'm not feeling like hearing her opinion right now. I guess, now that I think about it, that's why the ladies had been comparing notes about funeral makeup as they don't want snide comments from others, either. What a silly world we women have created for ourselves.

It's a quiet morning in Tucson Valley. The temperatures have already started creeping up over the week I've been here. It's 70 degrees at 9:00 in the morning.

Keat's flowers are blooming along the road as I drive to Jackie's Boutique, Mom's recommendation. *Keats*. My sitcom-named friend. It's nice to have a friend who isn't also a friend of Mom. It's nice to have a *male* friend who isn't Wesley. I shake away the thoughts from my mind. Why am I giving him any thought at all? I'm a 39-year-old divorcee. He's a 42-year-old hot landscaper who lives over a thousand miles from me with a million different reasons to never give me another thought after I leave.

I've sucked my mental energy level dry when I walk into Jackie's Boutique. Two heads pop up from the merchandise they are straightening when they see me. One of the women is Jan, *Jan with the nephew*. Was this a sabotage?

"Rosi! Hello! Your mother said you'd be coming in to see us today. She points to the other woman. "This is Vickie." A perfectly coifed woman with a dark tan and very skinny arms that stick out from her sleeveless dress waves her manicured fingers in the air.

"Ahh, I get it. Jan plus Vickie equals *Jackie's Boutique*."

"Yes!" Jan says, jumping up and down in excitement. "Isn't it the cleverest name ever?"

"Smart, Jan." I plaster a fake look of admiration on my face. How could Mom have done this to me after I listened so patiently to her unfurling secret last night? "I was hoping I might be able to find something simple to wear to Salem's funeral?" I assess the dresses that are hanging on the racks closest to me, a mixture of flower prints and bold colors. Doesn't anyone carry simple, black dresses anymore?

"Of course, Rosi. It's shocking, isn't it? I mean, no one liked Salem," she says, leaning close to me though no one else is in the store but Vickie. "Except for her suitors, of course. Do you think that maybe one of her jilted lovers…you know…*killed her*?" She gasps at her own words.

"Why would you think she'd been killed?" Does she have a source at the station, or is my mother the source of this information after I'd confided in her about what I'd heard when I was leaving the station yesterday?

"Honey, everyone in Tucson Valley knows that Salem was poisoned. Can you just imagine? Karen was listening to the police scanner when the call came in about Salem being found at the bookstore. Of course, they didn't say her name then, but who else would it have been? And then Vickie heard from her husband who plays golf with Officer Daniel's father that they'd found poison in her toxicology report. It's very shocking."

"Uh-huh. Officer Daniel's parents live in Tucson Valley?"

"Why, yes. His parents used to be prominent members of the Tucson Valley HOA, very important people. They bought a second house in Florida, though. We are quite lucky to have someone as fine as Officer Daniel working for us. He still lives in his parents' house here. They visit every once in a while. Isn't that the best? It's so smart to save money these days. He's a great son, taking care of their house when they're travelling."

That explains a lot is what I want to say, but instead I say, "That's great. I'm sure he's the best person to solve this case."

"Absolutely," she says, nodding her head up and down. "We can't have a murderer loose. Why, I wouldn't be surprised if it was someone that knew Salem very well, if you know what I mean. She had a lot of enemies."

Loose-lipped Jan keeps talking as I thumb through multi-colored capris sitting on a nearby table. "Whatever do you mean?" I ask sarcastically.

"She had many lovers, you know. Bob was heartbroken when she ended things with him. Whatever he saw in her I will never know, but he really loved her. Karen told Brenda who told me that she saw Troy Kettleman hanging out a lot at Salem's Stories. We all heard the rumors about the two of them. Who knows?"

"Did Salem have any family?" It's the first time that thought had occurred to me.

"She has a most ungrateful son from what I've heard," says Vickie, the first time she's spoken. "He'd come home maybe once or twice a year."

"And usually to get money," Jan adds.

"Then she'd been married before?" I ask, wondering if Zak will one day have a relationship with me where he only comes home once or twice a year when he needs something. The thought makes me sad.

"Salem? Nah, she's not the marrying type," says Vickie, her boney arms flailing about as she talks.

"She's a use-them-and-abuse-them type," Jan says dryly. "Now, let's find you that dress to pay your respects."

I clench my jaw as I follow her to the rack with the simplest dresses as I'd requested. Do these women realize they come across as having no compassion at all for a woman that's died?

"What size, dear? Ten? Twelve?" She looks me up and down.

"I'm between an eight and a ten though I guess it depends upon the designer."

"Oh, well that's good then. My nephew loves the skinny girls."

She hands me three dresses in size eight and one in size ten. I really wish I'd learned from Zak how to make a TikTok video because every time I'm around this incorrigible woman, I craft the most delectable stories to tell in my mind. I choose a simple, straight black dress that stops at my knees. I refuse a matching clutch purse as I don't plan to be holding anything I need to clutch. My regular purse will suffice.

"We'll see you at the service this afternoon, Rosi. Thanks for coming in today," says Vickie.

"Yes, indeed," says Jan. "You're going to be the prettiest one there. You don't look a day over forty. Allen is going to adore you! He's a CEO, you know." Her smile may be genuine, but I have a strong desire to wipe it off her saccharine face.

I don't even say goodbye as I let the door to Jackie's Boutique slam shut behind me.

Chapter 10

"Are you sure you don't need anything?" Mom asks Dad for the fifth time since I've been back from Jackie's Boutique.

"Renee, I have everything I want. Rosi made me a nice sandwich. You've filled my water bottle. I've been to the john. I've got my remote. I'm not disabled. If I need to get up, then I can. It will just take me a bit. The walker's right here if I need it," Dad says, slapping his hand on the handlebars of the walker.

"We won't be long. Well, the service may be a bit long. Cowboy Donnie is doing the service."

"Cowboy Donnie?" I ask as I pick Barley's hair from my dress. I'd made the mistake of saying goodbye to her after getting dressed.

"He's our preacher," says Mom.

"He wears a cowboy hat," says Dad.

"And he may have slept with Salem," Mom whispers.

"Renee!"

"Well, there are rumors, Richard."

I check the time on my watch. "Let's go, Mom. And please try to keep your true thoughts to yourself, at least for the next few hours."

"Fine."

A knowing look passes between us. I think she might regret having opened up to me last night.

The Tucson Valley Non-Denominational Church parking lot is packed. After dropping Mom off at the front door, I finally find a parking spot at the far end of the parking lot. I am rushing to the entrance of the church when I hear someone behind me.

"Hey! You dropped your sunglasses!"

I turn around to see Keaton standing in front of me and holding my sunglasses. "Hey, Rosi. Fancy meeting you here."

"Keats? Did you know Salem?"

"Everyone knew Salem." He winks at me.

I must look horrified because he starts laughing.

"Not like that! I do a lot of landscaping for the businesses on Main Street, so that's how I met Salem. I'm also a bit of a reader." He smiles, and I forget that I might be late to a funeral service.

"What's your poison?" I ask, throwing my hand over my mouth the minute the words have escaped. "I mean, what type of books do you like to read?"

Keaton laughs. "It's okay. I know about the poison rumors. I hope they aren't true, of course. She was not the most popular woman in the town, but she knew her books. I liked to look at the vintage books she'd put up for online auctions. I always got a sneak peek when I'd stop by."

"Hmm, I'd like to learn more about that, but we'd better get inside," I say, as the church bells strike eleven o'clock.

I don't dare sit with Keaton. Mom would have a fit. I slide into the end of the row where she is sitting with her friends. Jan nods her head approvingly. She is sitting with a handsome older man that must be her husband. He's wearing suspenders and a bow tie, an interesting choice for a funeral service.

"Dearly beloved, please stand," says a man at the front of the church who must be Cowboy Donnie. He is, indeed, wearing a cowboy hat. And cowboy boots, blue jeans, and a red and black plaid shirt. We stand to watch as a man about my age in a full suit and two women holding hands walk down the aisle and take their seats in the row closest to the casket.

"That is Salem's son, Barry, and her sister Sparrow and her *lover* Tina," Mom whispers—too loudly—into my ear.

"I think you might mean *wife*," I say. "It *is* the 2020s, Mom."

"Fine. Tina is Sparrow's *wife*."

"Shh," Jan says as she glares at me and scowls. Did she not see my *mother* talking, too?

After prayer, Cowboy Donnie gives the oddest soliloquy I have heard about someone at their funeral. He waxes on and on about her contributions to the community: bringing back a thriving bookstore to Tucson Valley, protecting vintage books from destruction, sharing of her means with a local cancer charity. But it's what he *doesn't* say that strikes me as odd. He doesn't mention her son or her sister or her sister-in-law. He doesn't mention *anyone* associated with Salem. He doesn't share one personalized story, even his own interactions with her. And after he is done and the guests have sung *Amazing Grace*, the service is over. No one else speaks. Her son and sister don't share stories of memories from the past. They don't even greet people at the door or allow anyone to extend their sympathies, yet there is not a single spot left open in the church pews. And from my vantage point, the only eye that's being wiped is Bob's who sits three rows up and across the aisle next to his grandson Devin who looks like he has at least combed his hair out of his eyes.

"That was lovely," says Mom as we walk toward her car.

I see Keaton getting into his truck. I push my fob and unlock the car. "Go ahead and get settled in the car, Mom. I think I left my sweater in the church," I say, turning around only when she's started walking.

"I don't remember you wearing a sweater," I hear her mumbling to herself, but she keeps moving in the direction of her car.

I walk over a couple of rows just as Keats starts his truck, a large blue pick-up truck, the kind that says *I'm a man*. "Hey!" I say, putting my hand on his windshield.

He rolls down the window. "Rosi, you scared me."

"Sorry! I just wanted to, uh, I wanted to ask you, uh…"

"Yes?" he asks quizzically, his eyebrows rising in unison, a gentle merriment dancing in them.

I am so bad at this. I haven't even considered being interested in another man, let alone dating, for more than twenty years. "I need some help…with…with pruning." I know how stupid I sound, but it's too late.

"Pruning?"

"Yes, my parents' shrubs are out of control, but I'm not sure how or when to prune them without making things worse."

"Would you like me to come by sometime?" Keaton doesn't stop smiling. "To…to prune your shrubs?"

"My parents' shrubs." I throw my hand over my mouth in horror, my lies getting me further and further into trouble. "Yes, please," I bite my lip, a nervous tick.

"Is this an emergency? Do you want me to come over now?"

"Oh, heck no! I mean, no thank you. It's not *that* big of a deal. I…I want to surprise my mom so it's best if you come by when she's not home."

"Okay, I'd be happy to prune the shrubs, *your parents' shrubs,*" he repeats, teasing me. "Give me your phone."

"My phone?"

He points to my phone that I am gripping tightly in my left hand. "So I can put my number in your phone so you can let me know when it's a good time to come over—when your parents aren't home."

"Oh, yeah. Of course, duh." I hand him my phone. And just like that I am a fifteen-year-old girl stumbling for words in front of a hot guy—only I'm leaving a funeral.

"Here you go," Keaton says as he hands me my phone.

"I'll be in touch," I say, neither of us turning to go.

We both look toward the front of the church when we hear loud voices. Bob is shouting something at another man, a contemporary in age though much taller with a cane that he is shaking in Bob's face. "What's that about?" I ask.

"That's Troy Kettleman," says Keaton.

"The man Salem was seeing?"

"You've heard those rumors, too?"

"I don't think there are many secrets left in this town," I say, recalling Mom's confession to me last night. And what would people think if they knew about that? "Do you think someone will intervene?" Troy is backing Bob closer to the outside wall of the church as he pushes his cane into his shoulder.

"Troy is the mayor, so I don't know if anyone will stop him from saying whatever it is he needs to say."

"Troy Kettleman is the *mayor?*"

"Yeah. And has been for a decade."

"Huh. Tucson Valley is getting more and more interesting the longer I'm here."

"That, Rosi, is an understatement," he chuckles. "I've got to get back to work. Give me a call when you'd like me to come over and help with your…pruning." He winks at me before driving away, leaving me blushing for the first time in a very long time.

Chapter 11

Officer Daniel called this morning to tell me that I was cleared as a suspect in the death of Salem Mansfield. Like there'd be any other conclusion? He'd also said he'd like to talk with me in person about another matter, so I am stopping by the station before picking Dad up from his post-surgery appointment at the doctor.

Officer Kelly waves when I walk into the station, greeting me with her chipper smile. Why can't I talk to her instead of dopey Officer Daniel? He walks toward me with his chest puffed out, trying to compensate in width for what he does not have in height.

"Ms. Laruee," he tips his imaginary hat.

"Rosi," I say.

"Fine, then. Rosi, thank you for coming down to the station."

"Of course, though I'm a bit confused. What do you need?"

Officer Daniel steals a look at Officer Kelly who raises her eyebrows at him with the first frown I've seen on her face. "Come with me, please."

I follow him through a maze of desks piled high with file folders. Have they not moved to the digital age yet? Even at the newspaper in Springfield, we've gone almost entirely digital, save for the few thousand people that still cling to a physical newspaper copy.

"Have a seat," Officer Daniel says, pointing to a cheap, fake leather green chair across from his desk where he sits in an office chair that rolls as he sits down. "So, I assume you are wondering why I've asked you here today."

"Yes," I say bothered by this unexpected addition to my day's schedule. "Do you mind getting to the point? I need to pick up my dad at his doctor appointment today."

Officer Daniel picks at his teeth with an overgrown thumbnail. I look away. "Your fingerprints were found on Ms. Mansfield's neck, where you'd taken her pulse."

"I know," I say, annoyed by this drawn-out charade.

"But while at the bookstore, my detective found…"

"Officer Kelly?"

"Yes, Officer Kelly found some evidence in the back of the store."

"What kind of evidence?" I ask, interested for the first time by anything this little man has to say.

"Oh, I can't possibly share that information with you. That would be quite unethical."

"Could you please get to the point?" I ask again.

"We have reason to believe that the circumstances leading to Ms. Mansfield's death were most nefarious."

"Nefarious?"

"Yes, *nefarious*. It means…"

"I know what nefarious means," I interrupt. "What circumstances about her death were nefarious?"

"That's the problem. I'm not sure, but we thought that you might be able to help us."

"Me?"

"Yes, well, *you* because you're staying with your mother."

"What does my mother have to do with this?" I can feel my palms sweating, so I clasp my hands together.

"More because of her connections."

"Can you just spit out what you're saying?" I look at my watch, as if I am about to be late for Dad's appointment though I have an hour before he finishes.

"Your mother has a gaggle of friends who seem to know everything that happens in this community even before the local police, and I need to know what *they* know about Salem and why someone may have wanted her dead."

"And you think that *I* can do what?" I stand up to leave.

"I need you to listen to their gossip and to tell me what you learn."

I am irate. "You mean that you want me to *spy* on my mother and her friends?" I put my hands on my hips and shake my head back and forth. "And why on earth would I do that—for you?"

"Because I know." He says it so quietly I can barely hear him.

"What?"

"Because I know why you left your job—why you were *let go*."

I push over Officer Daniel's pen container because it's the closest thing I can reach on his desk. I don't care how childishly I am reacting. "How dare you bribe me? How dare you look into my personal business?"

"And how dare you not tell your parents about why you're suddenly available to up and leave your life behind in Springfield?"

"How do you know that I haven't?" I lean in, challenging him to answer.

"Because at the funeral your mom would not stop talking about how proud she is of her daughter with the big journalist job. She doesn't know."

"You are a creep, Officer Daniel, a tiny, little jerk." I slam the office door behind me, stomp through the station—even as Officer Kelly tries to stop me—and drive away.

Chapter 12

"Can we go to the drive-thru at Dairy Queen, Rosi?" Dad asks after his good report at the doctor. "I feel like I could climb a mountain!"

"Don't get too crazy, Dad."

"You heard the doctor. He hasn't seen anyone at 70 who's progressed as nicely as I have at this point in the healing process."

"Let's start with ice cream and a walk down the block."

"I think I'm ready to take Barley for a walk!"

"Dad, Barley takes *me* for a walk."

"True, but she's a real cutie. Remember when you and Wes had that crazy cat? What was his name?"

"Glen."

"Ah, that's right. Whatever happened to Glen?"

"Wesley left the slider open, and he got out—never came back."

"Hmm, that's sad."

"It was a blessing. He was psychotic."

Dad laughs. "Do you miss him?"

"Glen? No, I told you he was psychotic." I shake my head as I recall being woken up with a paw in my mouth one morning when I'd dared to sleep in.

"No, Rosi—Wesley. Do you miss Wesley?"

I sigh. I'd hoped I'd be able to avoid the discussion of my failed marriage. "I'm doing fine on my own, Dad."

Dad squeezes my knee. "I know. You've been through a lot this year—the divorce, Zak going away to college and staying in Chicago to work for the summer. I imagine it's been a challenging transition."

"It hasn't been fun if that's what you're getting at."

"You know how your mother drives me crazy sometimes?" Dad grins devilishly.

"I've seen it a time or two," I laugh. "Why?"

"Well, even when she drives me crazy, there is no one on this earth I'd rather live my life with than her. If you *want* to, I hope that for you—someday—when you're ready. If you want to," he adds again. "not because you *have* to."

"I'll keep that under advisement."

"Thanks for being my ride."

"Always, Dad. Always."

After a nice lunch with my parents—salads because Mom is trying to use Dad's convalescence as a time to tinker with his diet, too—I go out to the patio to call Zak. He'd promised to be available today. He has a lot of his father in him, only wanting *to talk* when he's prepared and knows it's coming.

"Hey, Mom," he says after the third ring. "How are Grandpa and Grandma?"

"They are good. Dad had his post-op appointment today, and the doctor says he has knees like a forty-year-old, so he'd hyped."

Zak laughs and I yearn for his toddler belly laughs, when I'd made the best decision of my life and taken three years off from work to stay at home with him. I'd left my small-town newspaper job with no guarantee of being rehired, and Wesley questioned my decision every time the bills came due; but I'd managed to tune out his concerns and focus on our son for one of the most glorious times of my life. And somehow the bills always got paid. And when I'd returned to the workforce, I'd taken a pay raise and a new job in Springfield.

"Mom? Are you there?"

"Sorry, yeah. How is your internship?"

"It's great. I'm getting lots of experience. I'm part of a marketing team that's prepping for special events at the

United Center next year. I got to meet a couple of Chicago Bulls players who were in the building this week."

"That must have been exciting.'"

"When are you coming home?"

"I'm not sure. Grandpa still needs some help."

"Have you talked to the paper?"

I close my eyes and take a deep breath. "I'm not going back to the paper, Zak."

"Because they caught you," he says quietly.

"The paper let me go. It's true. Look, Zak, I'm not proud of what I did. It was a dark time in my life, and I made a poor choice."

"Dad says you didn't pay yet—you know, for slashing Cara's tires."

The sound of Wesley's lover's name on the lips of my only child is bristling.

"And you need to give him his portion of the house sale, Mom. It will be easier—on all of us. Please sell the house and be done with it."

"How do you know all of this?" I start tapping my flip flops on and off my foot in an anxious fury.

"Dad and I had lunch yesterday."

"And Cara?" I know the moment I've asked the question that I should have remained silent.

"Yes, Mom. She's a part of his life now. I'm worried about you. You need to…you need to find a new happiness."

My soul drops out of my chest as my pride and joy becomes the parent, telling me to get *over* the best part of my life. He's right, of course. But it hurts like a never-ending bad dream. "Can we change the subject?"

"No, Mom. We can't. You need to deal with your unresolved business. It's the only way you can move on."

I roll my eyes and crack my knuckles. "Are you sure you haven't become a psychology major instead of a marketing major?"

"Nope. My generation has our emotional garbage together."

"Okay, Zak. I'll talk to Dad. But I don't want you worrying about these things. Enjoy your internship and be a twenty-year-old, okay?"

"Love you, Mom."

"Love you, too."

Whoever said that parenting gets easier when your kid moves out clearly never had kids of their own. I pick

Barley up from her perch at my feet and hug her, appreciative for her unconditional love. She licks my face in appreciation.

Chapter 13

"Rosi, please join us for the game, won't you? Everyone is going to be there. I know that Jan is finalizing plans for her nephew's visit. Plus, Illinois is having a fantastic basketball season, so it will be a great game. And I'll need another set of responsible eyes watching over your dad as this is his first social outing since his surgery."

"Dad will be fine, Mom—nothing a beer or two can't fix." I smile, taunting my mother.

"That's what I'm afraid of," she sighs.

"I have some work to do first, but I'll stop over to the sports bar later. I promise." Mom and Dad met at the University of Illinois. Any chance they get to watch their beloved Fighting Illini play football or basketball, they are there. There is a large contingency of Illinois snowbirds in Tucson this time of year, so they've found a nice social group to watch the games with and even converted a few friends.

"Work for the paper?" Mom asks innocently.

"Mom, I…I…ugh," I exhale slowly.

"What's the matter, Rosi?"

I refuse to let Officer Daniel bribe me. Maybe Zak was right. I need to take care of my unresolved business. "I need to tell you something. And I need you to hear me without judgment. Do you think you can do that?"

Mom taps her hand absently against her leg. "Will I need a secret cigarette for this?" She smiles slyly.

"Maybe," I say, matching her smile. Learning about Mom's involvement with Salem and her secret coping mechanisms has humanized my mother in a way I didn't know was possible. And while Dad is in the shower, I tell her about the rage-filled night when I'd driven to Cara's job at the hospital, found her bright blue Toyota Rav4 and slashed every tire in a matter of minutes. I knew the moment I was done, stepping back to admire my work, that I'd made a horrible mistake, but there was no turning back. My boss was waiting in my office the next morning with a parking lot video recording shared by his wife—conveniently the hospital administrator—showing all of my handiwork. I'd begged the both of them not to go to the police. They'd only relented when my boss heard my end of a phone conversation with Cara where I agreed to pay for new tires. I'd begged Wes for his forgiveness. I didn't get it, though. I also lost my job. Not my finest moment.

"Wow." Mom sits on the couch. She pats the spot next to her for me to sit down, too. "I'm so proud of you, Rosisophia Doroche."

"Why would you say such a thing after what I've just told you?"

"Because Wesley did a shitty thing and…"

"Mom! I've never heard you swear!"

"And you also haven't seen me smoke a cigarette in decades or aid and abet a criminal." She raises her hands as if to say *what can I say?*

We burst into laughter and are still laughing when Dad wanders back into the room with his walker and wearing Illini orange and blue attire, head to toe.

"What are you two up to?" he asks, adding his smile to our merriment.

"We're laughing at how ridiculous that bandana looks around your neck!" I say.

"It's hot in Arizona! It's called an icy scarf. I can wet it and stay cool. Don't knock it until you try it, sassy girl!"

"It's still winter, Dad."

"I have options now." He moves the bandana back and forth across his neck. "Sometimes it gets hot watching the Illini play basketball. It can be so stressful."

"We have to go, Richard. Dinner at 5:00!"

"Have fun. I'll join you later."

Mom kisses me on the cheek and bends down to whisper into my ear, "You're doing it, Rosi. One foot in front of the other."

"Thanks, Mom."

When my parents have gone, I pull out my phone and text Wesley.

We can talk.

When a reply doesn't come right away, I go outside to water the new plants. It's while I am pulling weeds that I remember my conversation with Keaton at Salem's funeral and his offer to come over and help me with the landscaping. I check the time, 5:05, and wonder if he's still at work. I check my phone again. There is still no reply from Wesley.

I pull up Keaton's number and click *message*.

I know this is short notice, but if you're still in Tucson Valley, can you stop by my parents? To look at some plants. Thanks. Rosi

Sure. Send me the address.

The reply comes much quicker than I expected, and I have to work out what questions I can make up to ask him about my parents' landscaping. I wipe dog hair and dirt off my shorts and decide right away that was a mistake when it smears in a dark line down the front. I run inside, throw open the closet in the guest room, and choose a casual but clean blue t-shirt and a pair of khaki shorts that look like casual *I was just working in the yard clothes,* yet now they are clean. I pull my hair into a ponytail despite the fact that I feel too old for such a hairstyle, grateful for Grandma Kate's genes that didn't give her gray hair until she was in her seventies. So far, so good. And the sunglasses will hide the wrinkles. Why do I care? Why do I feel like I am a teenager again? The doorbell rings, bringing me back to reality. A handsome man waits outside the front door who thinks he is here to help with landscaping. Why is he really here? What am I going to say? What am I doing?

"Hey, Rosi," says Keaton as he stands in front of my parents' door with his water bottle in hand.

"Are you thirsty?" I ask, pointing at the water bottle. *Are you thirsty? Have I lost my mind?*

"Uh, yeah, I guess. The sun gets pretty intense by the end of my day. We were weeding in the downtown flower boxes today."

I look at his khaki pants that are covered in dirt along with a sweat stain on his gray t-shirt. Suddenly, I'm sweating, too. "Let's go out back, and I'll show you the plants I need help with…uh, pruning." I decide not to take Keaton through my parents' house lest Mom question any dirt on her carpet, so he follows me to the back gate. Barley is all over us the minute I close the gate.

"Is this one of Bob's puppies?" he asks as he squats down to pet Barley. Barley responds by rolling onto her back for belly rubs.

"How do you know Bob?" Barley licks my hand and then Keaton's.

"Everyone knows Bob. He's just a really friendly guy." Keaton stands up when Barley has settled at his feet.

"Then how on earth did he end up with someone like Salem—at least from what I've heard, of course?"

"Don't buy into everything the rumor mill has to offer. Bob sees the good in people, and he and Salem had a good run at it. I even double dated with them once."

"Oh. I didn't realize you were seeing someone. I mean, of course you're seeing someone. I mean, I certainly don't care if you're seeing someone. Why would *I* care if you were seeing someone? It's none of my busin…"

Just then Keaton brushes his lips softly across mine. "You can stop talking now, Rosi," he says, smiling. "Sorry, but I didn't know how else to put you out of your misery." His eyes swimmingly take in mine while I melt a little under the Arizona sun. "My companion on that double date was a first date for me. I'm not seeing anyone."

"Oh, well, that's great. Um, that's fine. I'm happy for you that…"

Once again, I don't stop Keaton as he presses his lips against mine. "Can I assume that you don't really need help with pruning?" He flashes a beautiful smile.

"I…I don't." My heart is beating so quickly I'm positive that Keaton can hear it. Barley barks at a chipmunk that runs across the patio. We both laugh, happy for the snap back to reality. "Keats, I'm…I'm newly divorced. I don't know what I am doing."

He takes my hand. "Well, I'm *oldly* divorced, so I can teach you a few things. Number one," he says, squeezing my hand, "You don't have to try so hard. I really enjoy your company. There aren't a lot of women out here who are my contemporaries in age. I like to date women who know the same pop culture references. I mean, you're an '80s sitcom kid, too, Rosi. Could we have a better connection than that? But more than that, you're easy to talk to. And you're a natural beauty. You don't have to try so hard to impress. You're just you."

I study Keaton's face. The wrinkles around his eyes are light, highlighted only by his deep tan. The laugh lines around his mouth are deeper, a sign that this man knows how to find the joy in life. Maybe I could learn a thing or two after all.

"What are you thinking?"

"Maybe this trip to Tucson Valley isn't so bad after all."

He grins. "Has it been bad up to this point?"

"Well, I did discover a dead body. That had apparently been murdered."

"Truth!" Keaton holds up his hand which reminds me of Zak when he'd take his Boy Scout pledges at meetings when he was in elementary school. "Do you think we could go on a proper date, Rosi—one where we don't have to pretend to like each other?"

This time I smile. "I'd really like that."

"And please let me know if you need help with *pruning*, if that's something you'd like." Keaton winks at me, and I blush.

"Let's have dinner first," I groan. "Oh no," I say, looking at the time on the sundial. "I'm supposed to meet my parents at the Tucson Valley Sports Club to watch the Illinois basketball game. I don't…I mean, I am not sure…"

Keaton grabs hold of my wrist. He lifts it to his lips and plants a gentle kiss on top of my hand. "Stop trying to explain so hard. "How about Sunday night? Can I pick you up for dinner then?"

I shake my head *yes* because I'm too overwhelmed to answer. And with a final pet of Barley, Keats walks back out of my parents' gate.

Chapter 14

"Hello, dear," says Paula when I sit down at the table with my parents' friends. I've ordered a hot dog and fries. Paula is shoving a brat into her mouth in a less than dignified way.

"Hi, Paula."

Jan leans in close to me, the brim of her orange and blue cowboy hat grazing my forehead. "Allen is so excited for your date next week. He's bringing you your own special pickleball paddle to use. The handle has sequins. Isn't that just adorable?"

"Look, Jan, I really can't…" A loud sound, like something heavy being dropped in the next room, catches our attention.

"You son of a…!" yells a man's deep voice.

"What on earth?" asks Mom.

I can tell Dad wants to jump up to check on the commotion, but he can't. I walk into the next room. Troy Kettleman is holding Bob Horace by the collar and pushing him against the wall. "You hurt her!" he yells at Bob. "You hurt Salem!"

Bob struggles to free himself from Troy's grasp before kneeing him in the crotch, causing Troy to stagger back toward the table. "I did no such thing. I loved that woman. You took her from me!"

"Then why did Officer Daniel find plastic bottles of poison in your garage?"

"What are you talking about?"

"Hey! Break it up!" yells Jan's husband Frank, who in bright orange suspenders and a polka-dotted bow tie, looks like the last person who'd be playing bouncer at a retirement community sports bar, but it works. Bob and Troy drop into the seats closest to each of them, their breathing coming in jagged breaths.

"The police are coming for you, Bob Horace. I promise you that you won't get away with what you did to Salem."

Bob leans forward, glaring at Troy. "And I promise you that *you* won't get away with what you did to Salem."

"What in tarnation do you think *I* did?" Troy's eyes dart around the room with nervous energy. "I cared about that woman!"

"You stole my sister's jewelry box," says the voice of a woman behind us.

We turn around to see Salem's sister Sparrow and her wife Tina standing in the sports bar and glaring at Troy.

"What are you talking about?" asks Troy. "I don't know anything about a silly jewelry box. Do I look like a jewelry guy?"

I have to give Troy that point as he's one of the few people in the bar dressed like a normal sports fan in blue jeans and an Illinois sweatshirt, an obvious Illini fan convert since he's the mayor of Tucson Valley and not a snowbird like most of the people here tonight.

"Somebody took my sister's jewelry box, and you were the last person who stayed in her home. I know so myself because Salem texted me the morning she died. She said you'd been over, and she'd ended things with you."

"Don't be ridiculous. I didn't take anything from Salem. All she did was cause me misery. Why would I keep a memento?"

"Wait a minute!" Bob stands between Troy and Sparrow. "Did you say that Salem told you she'd ended things with Troy?" But he doesn't wait for an answer and instead pivots to Troy. "Is this true?"

Troy's face drops. "She couldn't stop thinking about you, you brainless idiot." Troy spits on the floor by Bob's feet and walks out of the bar, the heels of his cowboy boots clicking against the cement floor.

Everyone from the dining room is now staring at Bob. Even Dad and his walker have wandered in with the excitement and commotion. Bob has a huge smile on his face. "I knew she still loved me," he says. "I knew it."

"Can we get back to the game now?" asks Frank. "It's two minutes to tip off."

"Yeah. Yeah, let's go everybody."

"Come on. Nothing to see here."

"That was something, huh?"

Mom and her friends return to the game leaving me alone with Salem's sister and Tina. Sparrow and Tina look more like twins than lovers, each wearing floor length maxi dresses with large flower patterns, Sparrow's in red and Tina's in purple. "I am very sorry to hear about your sister."

"Did you know Salem?" Sparrow asks, her face forming a frown. Tina rubs her back.

"No. I…I did shop in her store, though. It was lovely. And, um, I am the one that found her. I mean, I discovered her body."

A look of shock replaces Sparrow's frown. "How did she look?"

"Excuse me?"

"She said, *how did she look?*" repeats Tina.

112

"She, well, I...I checked her pulse. There was none."

"Did she look like she'd been harmed? Like obviously? That bumbling police idiot will only tell us that they found some *anomalies* in her system," says Sparrow.

"Oh. Officer Daniel. Yes, I've met him. I...are you sure you want the answers?"

"Salem was a difficult sister. She always wanted things her way. And she usually succeeded. She never approved of my relationship with Tina, but she was still my sister. And I'd like to know she didn't suffer some brutal killing."

"I can understand that." I nod my head before continuing. "To me, Salem looked like she'd fallen. There was some blood near her head and some sort of liquid near the middle of her body. But I didn't see any evidence that she'd been assaulted if that's what you mean."

Sparrow shakes her head up and down as if processing what I'd just told her. "I'm sorry to be so forward, but I am...well, I used to be a news reporter, and I heard you mention something about a jewelry box that's gone missing. Was there something valuable in that box that might be a clue as to what happened to your sister?"

"I think so," the wife says adamantly. "And we *thought* Troy might know something about it. That's why we came here tonight."

"But I have a good read on people," says Sparrow. "I'm a bit of a psychic."

She pauses for me to react, but I do not.

"And he was telling the truth. He doesn't know anything about the missing jewelry, and Salem was still in love with Bob."

"Huh." I drum the top of the table with my fingers. "This is an odd request, but I also collected the puppies she'd been watching for Bob at the bookstore, and when I went behind the counter to get their leashes and food, I noticed a desktop computer. Did the police happen to take the computer?"

"Officer Dorky didn't mention anything about the desktop. He said they'd taken a laptop in the back office which is where they found plastic beer bottles. Why?"

"Yes, Bob brewed beer at home, I believe. I was wondering if you might have a key to the bookstore that I could borrow to take a look at the computer, see if I can find any clues that Officer Daniel might have missed."

"You say you're a reporter?" asks Tina skeptically.

"I...yes, but not here. I'm visiting my parents from Illinois."

Tina looks at her wife who shrugs her shoulders. "I guess it can't do anymore harm. Will you let us know if you find anything that might help?"

"Yes, I will definitely be in contact. Here—here's my card." I reach into my purse and hand them my old business card from the newspaper though my number is current.

"Thanks," says Sparrow. "We are flying back to Nevada the day after tomorrow. "The key is hidden under the flower box on the window. It's in a magnetic box. Just feel around. You'll find it."

"Thanks. I'll be in touch."

"Oh, and Rosi?" She reads my name from the business card.

"Yes?"

"You've got a very orange aura," Sparrow says, staring intently at my face.

"Excuse me?"

"In my psychic experience, you carry an orange aura."

"What's that mean?"

"That, my dear, means that you are full of vitality and open to exploring your sexual and emotional being."

I raise my eyebrows in surprise. "That is *something*, isn't it?"

"Keep in touch."

And then they are gone. Cheering comes from the adjoining room telling me that Illinois must be scoring points in the basketball game. I reluctantly walk back into the room, my *aura* not at all aroused by my surroundings.

Chapter 15

I drive into town this morning with strict instructions about the brand of bread I am allowed to buy along with a list of equally specific items:

pork chops: quarter inch thick with little to no fat

bananas: four and green as possible

orange juice: some pulp, not-the-cheapest kind, not the most expensive kind

But first I am going to Salem's Stories. It will be a miracle if I can find the key under the flower box and get inside without anyone seeing me, which would only fire up the rumor mill.

I park down the street from Salem's Stories to scope out my best opportunity to get inside. The street is quiet at this time of day. After I've watched a couple walk into the coffee shop, I jump out of the car and walk nonchalantly toward Salem's Stories. One final quick sweep of the street, and I run my hand along the bottom of the flower box. I wonder if Keats and his crew are responsible for these pretty plants. *Focus, Rosi. Focus.*

I find the key box easily, pull it out, nod at an older man who is distracted by something on his phone as he passes by. Then I take the key from the box and let myself into Salem's Stories, locking the door behind me. The first thing I do is close the blinds so no one can look inside. I take a deep breath, reminding myself that I have the permission of next of kin to be here, well, at least almost next of kin as technically her son would be *that* person.

I assess the bookstore. Everything looks as it did the day I found Salem's body. Curiosity getting the better of me, I retrace my steps to where I found Salem lying on the ground. The spot is empty now, of course, save for a couple of stains on the floor. I get down on my knees to take a closer look. A dark burgundy stain has sunk into the olive-green carpet near where Salem's head had been lying. I'd thought at the time that she'd likely hit her head on the way down from whatever caused her to fall in the first place. The wet spot I'd seen near Salem's body has made another stain. A slight odor rises from the area, but I'm not crazy enough to put my nose to the carpet. It smells familiar though I can't place it.

I skirt around the imaginary outline of Salem's body and pass by a pile of books that appear to have been knocked over. Maybe by Salem's fall? Two books just outside of the larger pile lie splayed open on the floor in front of the open bathroom door. I pick up the first book and turn it over. The book is *The Great Gatsby* by F. Scott Fitzgerald. I'd read the book in high school, and this copy looks like it is much older than even *my* parents' high school days. The second book on the ground is a tattered copy of *The Tale of Peter Rabbit* by Beatrix Potter. Though I wasn't willing to smell the stains on the carpet, an unusual odor pulls me closer to the books for inspection. They have a strong smell of ammonia. That's odd.

I carry the books with me to Salem's office. It looks like it's been ransacked by Officer Daniel and Officer Kelly though I suppose Salem might also have been a messy packrat. The rest of the store is certainly overflowing with books in every nook and cranny. I spy some of the things Mom had confessed to bringing to Salem when she'd made a deal with her that she now regrets. My insecure mother had made a very poor decision to help a manipulating, ill-intentioned woman—all because of an ill-perceived threat to her marriage and those of her friends' marriages because of an overly charming bookstore owner.

A sound from the front of the store startles me. Who else has keys? Is Sparrow here? I step out of the office and duck behind an aisle of books—westerns. I lean against the Zane Grey novels to try to get a view of the front counter. The only light coming in filters in through the front door. I'd been careful not to turn on the lights. I can see the silhouettes of two men who are about the same height. They walk behind Salem's desk. One of them turns on her desktop computer. I walk closer, edging along the Harlequin romance books now, almost tripping over a stack of books with bare-chested men. The men look up when *Logger Lover* falls to the ground. I freeze until they return to looking at the computer. One of them hunches over as if writing something down followed by the sound of a piece of paper being ripped from a notepad. When they turn to walk toward Salem's office, I have to throw a hand over my mouth as I gasp. One of the men is Barry, Salem's son. I'd only seen him at the funeral, nothing remarkable standing out about the man who appeared to be around my age, maybe a bit older. His hairline is receding, and he has a pooch around his waist, maybe a beer belly, though I don't imagine Salem's son would be anything but a drinker of the finer liquor. I watch him walk into the office, closing the door behind him. The other man isn't really even a full-grown man but Bob's teenage grandson Devin.

It's my chance to escape unnoticed, but I can't stop myself from doing one more thing, the thing I'd wanted a lot more time to do. I walk behind the counter where Barry and Devin had just been. The computer monitor is still on. I wiggle the mouse so that it does not go blank and perhaps require a passcode to access. I squint at the screen, wishing I'd brought my reading glasses. On the screen is an email. I read through it quickly.

Ms. Mansfield,

I am most unhappy with the recent transaction regarding the sale of The Hobbit by JRR Tolkien. The book arrived last week as I indicated in my first email to you. If you do not rectify this situation immediately, I will be forced to approach the proper authorities. Forgery of any kind is criminal, but to forge a beloved book is sinful. You should be ashamed of yourself.

James Nottingham

I write down Mr. Nottingham's name and email address. I hit the back button. A row of emails that say *Payment Sent* in the subject field catch my attention. I click on the top email. A woman named Nanette Collins had sent payment of $14,000 for a copy of *The Great Gatsby*.

That Great Gatsby? I write down Nanette's name. The date of the email is from three days ago. I hear the office door open, grab the paper with my notes, squat down, and nearly crawl out the front door. I run toward my parents' car as soon as I'm free and sit next to my front door and out of view in case Barry or Devin decides to check the street. I stay there for ten minutes before I trust it's safe to get back into the car.

Chapter 16

I am still trying to process what I'd just learned at Salem's Stories. Salem was, in fact, creating counterfeit books to sell through her shop online. All of the things Mom had bought for her so that Salem herself could not be traced for having purchased the items: ammonia, tea bags, special ink, etc. were among the things I imagined were in her office. To the untrained eye, they'd look like random items dispersed amongst a very messy office, but knowing what I know now, the tea bags were for aging paper with brown spots. The ink was for mimicking words, the various types and thicknesses of paper for recreating the look of pages from old books. The ammonia likely had some sort of chemical effect on paper though I don't know what exactly. And Mom had said she was convinced that Salem was forging vintage books to look real after doing her own internet search of the items Salem had asked her to purchase. She'd only agreed to help with the purchases when she was cornered one day in the bookstore buying her niece a book for her baby shower. Mom only agreed to help Salem because she thought she'd be in Salem's good graces and then she'd leave her husband and the husbands of her friends alone—away from her seductive web of marriage meddling.

And when she'd confronted Salem about her suspicions, Salem sent her a digital link to a hidden camera file that showed Mom dropping the items for the forgeries off to Salem at the front desk. If Mom went to the police with her allegations about Salem, then she'd be implicated for helping her with the crimes because that's sure as heck what Salem would tell Officer Daniel. And he'd believe it, too, I assume as the more I learn about Salem the more I believe she can cast a spell on the men in her life. Obviously, her son is continuing her schemes. Why else would he have been in his mother's office today and viewing the computer with the emails about vintage book sales? But why was Devin with him?

I am hoping that Mom is home because I can't keep all this information to myself. But I wonder how angry she will be at me for *poking my nose in it* as she'd say when I asked too many questions as a kid. When I turn onto my parents' street, I am surprised to see a car in the driveway. Usually, guests are announced in advance. Mom likes to make sure the house looks perfect. I'm even more surprised to see a rental company sticker on the back of the car.

I catch my breath the moment I walk into my parents' living room. I smell him before I see him, the familiar aftershave of my ex-husband wafting in my direction. Wesley is here. Wesley is here in Arizona. In my parents' house. Right now. My shoulders tighten involuntarily, and I clench my jaw. I put on my figurative mask, plaster a fake smile on my face, and walk to the dining room where he is sitting with my parents. Same old Wesley, baseball cap on backwards hiding the beginnings of his receding hairline, day-old stubble on his face, the same chiseled cheekbones that attracted me to him so many years ago.

"Hi, Rosi," he says with an equally fake smile on his face. "Surprise!"

All I can do is nod my head in agreement. Surprise indeed! I concentrate on opening and closing my hands into fists, another therapy relaxation tip. "Hello, Wesley. I didn't expect to see you today. Were you just in the neighborhood?" I ask sarcastically.

"Something like that." He slides a piece of paper across the dining room table.

Mom looks at Dad who looks at me. "We'll let the two of you talk in private," Dad says. "Renee, let's check on Barley."

"Yes, let's do that."

We both watch Mom and Dad shuffle to the patio, Barley jumping up on both of them the moment they step outside. "When did your parents get a dog?" Wesley asks.

"It's my dog," I say dryly.

Wesley raises one eyebrow, a habit I grew to hate over our twenty years together as it always indicated judgment over something I did or said. "I thought you considered dogs too much of a burden for your *busy* life."

I wish I could smack the grin off his face. Open hand. Clench fist. Open hand. Clench fist. "I have more time for a dog now. They are more amenable than a husband." I glare across the table and wait for his response.

"If you mean that dogs can be controlled and suffocated easier than a spouse, you are correct. I'm happy for you." He doesn't smile. Nor do I.

"Why are you here? In Arizona? Fifteen hundred miles from home?"

Wesley takes a slow, deep breath. "Cara and I are vacationing in Vegas this week."

I bristle on the inside at her name, a tiny atom bomb going off in my chest, but I don't show it.

"So, we decided to drive down here for the day because you and I have some business to attend to." He slides the paper between us a bit closer so that I have no choice but to look at it.

"What is this?" I pick up the paper and see the letterhead of his expensive lawyer at the top.

"Cara and I are trying to buy a new home. And we'd like to make a larger down payment. You need to sell the house. And this is my final offer for how the purchase price can be divided. I'm not agreeing to a 60/40 split, Rosi. I know you owned the house before we were married. I know Grandma Kate was a very special person. But I put a lot of money and sweat equity into the house, too. We lived in the house for nearly the same number of years. So, this is my final offer."

"Or what?"

"What do you mean?" he asks, irritated.

"This is your final offer…or what?"

"Accept these terms, or I'm taking you to court."

I nod my head silently up and down, processing Wesley's newest threat. *Give me space, or I'm going to leave. Give me more visitation with Zak, or I'll sue for custody. Give me the Audi, or I'll ask for the pinball machine, too*—the pinball machine my dad had restored for my twenty-fifth birthday, a thoughtful gift eliciting nostalgia from our time together in the local bowling alley. I read through the document. Wesley is offering a 53/47 split with not an even number in sight. I want to crumple the paper into a ball and throw it in his face. No. I *really* want to crumple the paper into a ball and shove it into his mouth. But then I remember Zak and how he'd begged me to handle my *unresolved business* as he'd called it, and suddenly I have no more desire to fight. "Do you have a pen?" I ask.

"Huh?"

"Do you have a pen so that I can sign your paper?" I ask annoyed.

"You're…you're going to sign it?" His eyes widen in surprise.

"Isn't that why you are here, Wes?"

"Yes, of course. I just…I thought there might be a bit more of a fight…"

"I don't want to fight anymore," I sigh.

"I don't want to fight either, Rosi." He reaches into his bag that hangs on his chair and pulls out a pen. "Here you go."

I sign the document and slide it across the table. "The extra percentage you took can pay for Cara's tires."

He looks like he is about to complain but closes his mouth. Instead, he shakes his head in agreement. Wesley sits, staring at the signed document for a moment before speaking. "Thanks, Rosi. I really wish you the bes…"

I put up my hand to stop him. "Don't embarrass yourself. Just go."

He stares at me for a moment before getting up. "Okay. Please tell your parents goodbye for me." When he gets to the front door he turns around and stares at me again for a moment too long.

"It's time to leave, Wesley."

"I wish you well, Rosi. And…and I want you to know that I really did love you."

He just couldn't help himself. "Yes, I know, Wes. Sleeping with your co-worker is the sweetest way to show your love for your wife. Get out."

And after he has closed the door behind him and started his car, I lean against the door, letting myself slide to the ground where I cry my eyes out.

Chapter 17

Mom and Dad have smothered me with attention since Wesley left this afternoon. I do appreciate their care, and truth be told, it's kind of nice to be parented like I was when I was nine and didn't make the softball team. They'd let me have two helpings of ice cream then and watch all my favorite cartoon videotapes even though Dad had to miss the Chicago Cubs game on television. While I didn't get ice cream or cartoons today, Mom made me a strawberry banana smoothie and binge watched three episodes of House Hunters with me. Even Dad played along choosing the wrong house for the couple each time. But I need to get out of the house and to clear my head now.

"I'm taking Barley for a walk. I'll be back in a bit."

"That's nice, dear. Fresh air will be good for you," says Mom.

"Don't forget the dog treats. Barley likes her treats," says Dad.

"Got it," I say, smiling. I feel guilty for making my parents so concerned about me. It's time to put my big girl panties on now.

Barley is thrilled to go for a walk. It's overcast this afternoon, but the air is warm enough that I don't need more than a light jacket. I decide to walk in the direction of Bob's house. Barley might like a visit with her siblings. Bob's garage is open as I approach his house, another house that looks like all of the others in the neighborhood. He is tinkering with his homemade beer, wearing a bandana around his forehead though it's not hot enough to sweat.

"Hey, Bob!" I wave from the sidewalk. I slip Barley a treat, and she sits at my feet.

He looks up, surprised to see Barley and me. "Rosi? Hi!" His face lights up. "How are you on this gloomy winter day?"

"Gloomy?" I say, arching my eyebrows in surprise. "You don't know a gloomy winter day until you've lived through a Midwest winter. It's still delightful to me."

"Ahh, perspective. You're right. My days living in Michigan were very many years ago. Silly me. I do remember those cloudy, snowy, cold days. Did you know that I've lived here full time for ten years now?"

"I didn't know. How do you handle the summer heat?"

"Air conditioning," he chuckles. "And the pool. I put in a pool about six years ago. It's a lifesaver. Plus, Suzi loves the pool." At the sound of her name, Suzi raises her head from her dog bed in the corner of the garage. Barley paddles over to her mother, lets herself be licked, and collapses against her side in the dog bed.

"Where are the puppies?"

"The puppies are gone," he says sadly. "All sold. But that's a good thing—little mini-Suzis spreading joy to other families."

"That's nice, but I imagine your house is a lot quieter now."

Bob stares past me, and for a moment I think he's sad about the puppies, but when he doesn't stop staring, I turn around to follow his gaze. A police car is pulling in front of his house with Officer Daniel in the driver's seat.

"Suzi, stay," Bob commands Suzi who obediently drops back to her dog bed after sitting up with the noise of the police car. I coax Barley back to my side and slip her another treat while holding onto her leash.

"Bob," nods Officer Daniel as he walks up the driveway. "Rosi," he says, lingering too long on my face for my liking. He twists a finger around the front of his belt loop as he approaches.

"What can I do for you, Officer Daniel?" Bob asks, eyeing him suspiciously. There are no more smiles on Bob's face. It's clear the two men do not care for each other.

"I was hoping to speak with you...*alone*," Officer Daniel says as he looks at me again.

"I told you everything I thought might be helpful the last time we talked. I don't have anything to hide from anyone—and that includes Rosi. Whatever you've got to say, say it."

Officer Daniel shakes his head up and down. "In that case, Bob Horace, I'm here to arrest you for the murder of Salem Mansfield." He grabs hold of Bob's arm and pulls it roughly behind his back. He attaches handcuffs to each of his wrists. "You have the right to remain silent. Anything you..."

"What are you talking about?" yells Bob, the veins on his forehead throbbing. "I didn't kill Salem! I loved Salem!"

"I have evidence that you were the last person seen going into her store before her death," says Officer Daniel.

"I was there. I don't deny it. I was taking the puppies. Didn't anyone see the puppies? Salem was my puppy sitter."

"And why exactly did you need a puppy sitter if you are retired, Mr. Horace? Your lies won't work anymore."

Bob hangs his head as Officer Daniel starts walking him to the car. "You're wrong! I'm not lying about anything!"

"Wait! You can't do this! Bob didn't kill Salem!" I yell, but Officer Daniel ignores me.

Bob turns his head to speak to me. "Rosi, can you take care of Suzi until I get this all straightened out?"

"Of course! I'll keep her. Shall I call you a lawyer?" I yell, but Bob is already closed into the backseat of Officer Daniel's car.

Before getting into the front seat, Officer Daniel looks at me with a smug face. "Perhaps you should choose your friends more carefully, Ms. Laruee."

I don't know how long I stand on Bob's driveway before I start moving again. It's Barley's whining that catches my attention first. "I know, girl. I know. Let's go get your mama." I find a leash in Bob's garage and attach it to Suzi's collar. I pick up her dog bed and tuck it into my armpit because I'm guessing she's loyal to her bed. I open Bob's car to get his garage door clicker, lead the dogs down the driveway, and push the close button. Suzi and Barley can't get enough of each other. It is a much longer walk back to my parents' house with the two of them tangling their leashes than it was when I walked with just Barley to Bob's house. My head is swimming with questions. This has been the longest day. First, Wesley and now this.

I take the dogs into the backyard through the gate at the back of the house. After taking long drinks from Barley's dog bowl, they collapse into a heap from exhaustion onto the hard cement patio.

"What do we have here?" asks Mom who is opening the sliding back door.

"This is Suzi," Barley's mother. "She's Bob's dog."

"Why do you have another one of Bob's dogs?" Mom asks as she bends down to pet the two dogs who are on their way to slumberland.

I sigh and shake my head from side to side. "I'm not sure you're going to believe me, but I have so much to tell you."

"I think a day like this requires margaritas. Does that sound good to you?"

"You don't even know the half of it!"

Dad follows Mom outside when she comes back with a pitcher of margaritas. He's carrying the glasses in the bag that hangs from the front of his walker. I'm not sure he's ever going to give that thing up even when his knee has healed.

"Okay, let's hear it," Mom says as she raises her glass. "Cheers to gossip!"

Dad smacks his head but lifts his glass anyway. I join in.

"Let me start at the end and work backwards," I say. "I'm skipping the middle because that was *his* surprise visit, and I have no intention of speaking that man's name any more than I have to."

Mom leans forward as if she is about to receive the biggest piece of news she's ever gotten. Just then her phone dings. She picks it up to read the message. Her eyes get big. "Bob Horace was arrested for Salem's murder?"

Dad chokes on his margarita, and all I do is hang my head and close my eyes. News travels fast in the Tucson Valley Retirement Community.

"There's no way that sweet man could have harmed Salem. I never understood what he saw in her as a partner, but he wouldn't have *killed her!*" says Mom as she stares at me.

"I was there when Officer Daniel arrested him."

"Did he say *why?*"

"He said that he had Bob on video as the last person in the bookstore—before me, that is."

"Which means that you were the *next* person in the store since you found her body?" asks Dad.

"Exactly."

"Well, thank goodness that dimwit police officer didn't blame *you* for Salem's murder," Mom says as she fans herself with her free hand that is not holding her margarita glass.

"Eek! I hadn't considered that."

"What can we do for Bob?" Mom asks as she strokes Suzi who has picked up her own dog bed to lay on Mom's feet with Barley curled up against her mom.

"There's more. I told you I was going backwards, and I haven't told you yet about the start of my day."

"Goodness gracious. I may need two margaritas."

"Pace yourself, dear," Dad says as he pats Mom's arm.

"I had a suspicion that there may have been something funny going on in the bookstore, when Salem was alive." I shoot Mom a quick look and a wink to assure her that I am not going to tell Dad about her secret, so she knows not to ask too many questions.

"Suspicions about what, Rosi?"

"Salem seemed secretive," I lie, "and I asked her sister Sparrow if I could have permission to enter Salem's Stories and check things out for myself."

"That's my reporter daughter using her skills," Dad says, beaming.

It crushes my soul a bit to see him so proud about a job I once held—until I slashed my husband's lover's tires and got fired. I take a deep breath and continue. "Sparrow told me where to find the key. I locked myself in the bookstore and was retracing my steps the day that I found Salem's body when I heard the front door opening."

"Oh my!" Mom clutches her chest, her eyeballs the size of Grandma Kate's teacup saucers from the set I'd use to have tea parties with my dolls.

"I hid behind the stacks."

"Who was it, Rosi? Who was in the store?" Dad leans forward, both of my parents hanging on my every word.

"Barry, Salem's son."

"Well, that's not odd," Dad says disappointed.

"He wasn't alone." I pause for drama as the storyteller in me is enjoying my captive audience. "Bob's grandson Devin was with him."

"Devin? Why would he be with Barry?" asks Mom.

"I don't know, but I watched Barry do something on the desktop computer before walking with Devin to the back office. When they were in the office, I ran to the computer."

"That was so dangerous, Rosi—if you think they were up to something illegal."

"What did you discover?" asks Dad.

"There was an email, several emails actually."

"About what?" asks Mom. I shake my head quickly back and forth hoping she will be reminded to not ask too many questions now.

"The emails seemed to show that Salem had been selling vintage books over the internet…"

"Everyone knew that," Dad says. "There was a big ad in the program at the civic center when we saw the Buddy Holly cover band."

"But she wasn't just selling *any* vintage books. She was selling *forged, counterfeit* vintage books, and at least one customer called her out on it…in an email."

"Damn," says Dad.

"Richard, the swearing! Oh my, that's quite awful, isn't it? I mean, who would do such an unscrupulous thing?" Mom is laying the drama on thick. I shoot her a look to cut it out. Her face is red, and she drops her chin to her chest and takes a deep breath.

"But I don't understand. What was Barry doing with that information?" Dad asks.

"I am guessing that he was continuing his mother's scheme."

Chapter 18

I'm lying in bed scrolling through my phone. Barley is asleep at my feet, snoring softly. She's allowed in my room at night when the door is closed. Otherwise, she'd be tripping Dad up which isn't a great idea with a recovering knee. Suzi thinks my bed is *her* bed and has decided to make the most of the large space by spreading out in the middle of the bed. I am too wired to sleep even though it's well past midnight. My simple plan was to take a break from the chaos of my life in Illinois by taking care of Dad after his surgery. Instead, I've traded one chaotic, confusing life for another. In the matter of a week and a half, I've discovered a dead body, adopted a dog, kissed a man who wasn't Wesley, and possibly uncovered an expensive book counterfeiting scheme.

A loud sound startles me. It comes from outside my window. I remember my conversation with Dad when I first arrived about being aware of javelinas—small, wild boar-like creatures that populate this part of Arizona. They are supposed to be as scared of us as we are of them, but I don't think I'd like to test that theory. Dad had shared a story about how a baby javelina had fallen into a garbage can outside their neighbor's house and cried wildly all night long until the next morning when the neighbor tipped the can over and freed him. I shudder to think about a pack of javelinas being on the other side of the wall, but it's not squealing I hear. It sounds like something metal rolling down the driveway. Then a car engine starts up, casting light across my bedroom wall from the headlights as it drives away. The population of Tucson Valley Retirement Community is not known for middle of the night drive-bys.

I lie in bed for another five minutes before my curiosity wins out. I slip on my crocs and put on my glasses. It's too late for contacts. Barley rolls over, annoyed by my movement, but I'm not going outside alone. I may be a grown woman, but I still know when I need a guard dog though Barley doesn't really emit a fierce protector vibe. Suzi is much too comfortable in the bed to be bothered by middle of the night noises. I put a leash on Barley's collar, coax her onto the floor, and tiptoe to the front door, checking to make sure that my parents' bedroom door is closed.

The streetlight in front of my parents' house is shining brightly as are the many streetlights spaced evenly along the road. Keaton has told me that part of his team's responsibility is to maintain spring flowers around the poles. That's a lot of flowers to care for, especially when you work in a desert. At the end of the driveway, something reflects the light from above. Barley follows me slowly, irritated by the disruption in her sleep. It's a can. I pick it up—spray paint. I look around, but there doesn't appear to be anyone lurking in the shadows. And I *had* heard a car drive away when I was still in the house. I walk toward my parents' car which is parked in the carport. And then I see it, in bold green letters.

Stop snooping

The can slips out of my hand and rolls back down the driveway. Barley barks loudly. I crouch down to pet her. "It's okay, girl. Shush. You'll wake the neighborhood." She rubs her head against my hand. "Sorry. I don't have any treats this time of day."

If I couldn't sleep before, I *really* can't sleep now. There's no sense calling the police. They can't do anything now, and I am certainly not going to wake up my parents. I check the time. It's 1:00 in the morning. I sit on the front steps, scanning the street, but I'm confident that whoever left this message is not coming back tonight. I stare at my phone considering what I want to do. I click on Keaton's name in my contact list.

Are you up?

I regret it the second I have sent the message and am about to activate the delete option, a new iPhone update, when I receive a reply.

Yep. Binging old episodes of Dexter.

Cool.

You like serial killers, too?

Not really.

Everything okay?

Not really.

??

Sitting outside my parents' house with Barley. Someone spray-painted their car.

WTH?

Yeah.

With words or pics?

Words.

What does it say?

Stop snooping.

That's bad.

Yep.

I'm coming over.

No! You have to work tomorrow.

Doesn't matter. I'll be right there.

"What have I done, Barley?" She licks the top of my Crocs and closes her eyes. I hug my body with my arms. It's a chilly night, and I hadn't planned on stepping outside when I put on my green tank top and pajama bottoms. I touch my hair which feels like a bird's nest, piled high on top of my head since I hadn't removed the elastic band from my ponytail. I reach for my phone to text Keaton back, but he's pulling up in front of the house right now with his blue truck. I take a deep breath before tying Barley's leash to a metal peacock that is staked in the ground near a golden barrel cactus. I wish it could tell me what happened tonight. Barley is so tired she doesn't even bark when Keaton walks up the driveway—some guard dog she is. I throw my arms across my chest as I suddenly realize I'm not wearing a bra. "Hey," I say. "I'm sorry for dragging you out here in the middle of the night."

Keaton has a huge smile on his face, a welcome comfort that doesn't exactly match the mood of the night. "There is no way I'd pass up the chance to help a snowman in distress—especially in Arizona. Snowmen are hard to come by."

I cock my head to the side and wrinkle my forehead in confusion. "What do you mean?" I ask at the same time Keaton points to my face. I close my eyes and wish I could click my crocs three times and disappear. "It's a face mask," I say softly.

"I'm only teasing you, Rosi. You look cute."

"I...I...I'm...oh man, this was a bad..."

Keaton reaches for my hand, but I don't dare unleash the hold on my floppy boobs. "You're adorable, with or without the white face mask." He bops me on the nose, taking some of the cream off and wiping it on the end of his nose. "Now we are a snow couple!"

I bite my top lip. "I think I'm in the middle of a nightmare."

"Well, I'm happy to have a role in your dreams." He smiles, and for a moment I have completely forgotten why I've brought Keaton here.

I point toward my parents' car. "Want to see?"

I follow Keaton to the car, hugging myself tightly. In green printed letters—*Stop Snooping*—is prominent. "Do you have any suspects?"

"I think it might be the artwork of Salem's son."

"Barry?"

"Do you know him?"

"He's a real tool. He used to live in Tucson Valley, but the town proper, not the retirement community, and sometimes my crew works there. He took us to court a few years ago. He accused us of cutting his cable line when we were doing some landscaping for the city. There were no cable lines anywhere near where we were working, but my boss at the time settled with Barry out of court to save us the embarrassment of more mudslinging that might threaten future contracts. He was looking for a chance to upgrade his cable without having to pay. I'm convinced of it. But why on earth do you suspect Barry of vandalizing your car?"

I tell him the story about spying on Barry and Devin in the bookstore. He listens intently and doesn't interrupt me until I am done talking.

"I thought you said he didn't see you."

"He didn't, but Officer Daniel let it slip that Salem's Stories had a security system, at least at the front door, so I imagine he saw me on the video camera. Those things are usually digital nowadays."

"You have to tell the police. This might help Bob—turn the investigation another direction."

"I know. Tomorrow—or least in a few hours. I appreciate you coming over. I guess I needed a friend. It was unnerving."

"I'm glad you called." Keaton takes his thumb and wipes away a clear spot on my right cheek. He leans close and plants a gentle kiss on my face, and I tingle all the way to my toes. As Keaton walks away, he turns around and yells, "You can release your breasts now!"

I hear him laughing as he gets in his car to drive away. I am both mortified and instantly turned on.

Chapter 19

Officer Kelly stands outside my parents' house assessing their car. My parents are standing behind me. They'd been most disturbed to hear that there had been vandalism in Tucson Valley and most distraught that it had happened in *their* driveway to *their* car. She snaps some pictures of the vandalism, the *Stop snooping* even easier to read in the daylight. She bags the spray paint can that I'd picked up from the end of the driveway. "You really should have left the can there. Now it may be harder to check for fingerprints."

"Yeah, sorry. I wasn't thinking clearly in the middle of the night."

"She was terrified, Officer Kelley," says Mom, putting her arm around my shoulders like I am her little girl again.

"I understand, Mrs. Laruee. Can you think of anything else that might be helpful, Rosi?"

She smiles at me, and I remind myself how grateful I am that it is Officer Kelly and not Officer Daniel who is taking my statement this morning. "Well, there is something that might help, but, uh…" I hesitate. "It might not be related."

"We can assess if the information means anything. Go ahead." She smiles again, and her kind eyes make me feel a little less crazy for what I am about to say. I take a deep breath.

"Go on, Rosi. Tell her." Dad nods his head in agreement.

"I had some suspicions about Salem's vintage book sales, the ones she'd sell online. I'm not sure why." I don't dare mention Mom. "Anyway, I talked with Sparrow, Salem's sister, and she gave me permission to enter the store. While I was there—in the back—I saw Barry Mansfield enter the store. He looked at something on the computer that I later confirmed to be emails about the book sales including one from an angry buyer who accused Salem of forgery. I think they may have been working together, and I'm guessing he saw me on a security camera at the store, the same one that Officer Daniel saw Bob Horace on. And he wanted to leave me a message."

Officer Kelly laughs so hard that all my parents and I can do is stare at her with our mouths hanging open.

"Excuse me, but I don't understand what's so funny about this."

"I'm sorry. I'm laughing because this isn't the first time I've heard about the possibility of Salem counterfeiting books, and it is simply ludicrous. I've investigated the matter thoroughly; I can assure you."

"But what about the emails?" asks Dad who has graduated from his walker to using a cane.

"Those come often. Salem has shown me many. They are simply customers with buyer's remorse. Some husband or wife spends thousands of dollars on a *book*—can you just imagine—and then the spouse gets angry and so they accuse Salem of creating a fake book in an attempt to get a refund."

"But I don't understand. Why would Salem show you the customer emails when they are accusing her of a crime?"

"For just that reason. She wanted someone in authority to know that she was being threatened."

"Well, if that is the case, then why aren't the senders of those emails suspects in Salem's murder and not Bob?"

"Because Bob was the last one to see Salem alive. We have it on video, Rosi. It's hard to deny."

"But Salem died of poisoning. She wasn't bludgeoned or strangled to death. Anyone could have poisoned her at another time, right?"

"Look, I know you have a softness in your heart for Bob because of that cute pup over there," Officer Kelly says, pointing at Barley who is staring at us through the slats in the back fence along with Suzi. "Bob is our main suspect, but we don't have enough evidence to charge him with murder—yet. He's being released today."

"What a relief," says Mom.

"I think I'd best be going," says Officer Kelly. "If you can think of any *other* theories, please don't hesitate to reach out. And as far as getting that car painted, there's a shop on Front Street that does a great detailing job. You should check it out."

"Thanks. I'll do that."

"You might want to be careful, too. Watch out for yourself."

Mom starts fanning herself with her hands. "Oh my. Oh my."

I put my arm around *her* shoulders this time. "It's okay, Mom. Don't worry. Thanks for coming out this morning, Officer Kelly. You are so much more pleasant to deal with than Officer Daniel."

She pats my arm. "He doesn't even need to know I was here. I'll take care of you."

When she is gone, my parents and I walk into the backyard. Suzi has quickly become used to the treats that Dad hides in his pocket, so I have to restrain her until he is seated.

"What do you think about Officer Kelly's theory about the counterfeit books not being valid?" asks Dad.

"I think it's odd. I don't understand. Why would Barry have seemed so interested in those emails? What was he doing in the office? And why was he even there?" So many things don't add up.

"Hello? May I come in?" A voice calls out over the fence into the backyard.

Suzi is the first one to greet Bob with wet, sloppy kisses. Barley follows her mother. I trust the judgement of dogs, and they approve.

"Bob, please sit down," says Dad, pointing to an empty chair at the patio table.

"It's so good to see you, Bob. How have you been? Did they treat you okay?" Mom asks. "Let me get you some water."

Bob puts his hand on top of Mom's. "I'm fine, Renee. Just stay here. Thank you, though. And thank you for taking care of Suzi. I'm really sorry to have put you all in this position."

"You didn't put us in any position. Look at my puppy! She adores having her mama here." Now that Bob has been properly greeted, Barley and Suzi have retreated to sharing Suzi's dog bed, Barley's head resting on Suzi's back.

"I just can't believe they'd arrest you with nothing more than a view of you dropping off your puppies at the bookstore as their only reasoning," says Mom.

"I can't rightly understand it, either."

The three of us sit quietly for a moment. It's not like we are long lost friends. Bob and Salem didn't run in Mom and Dad's social circles. Salem wasn't part of the Gossip Club. And I've only been here for a week and a half. A nagging question in my mind gets the best of me, a reporter's mind that never quits—even without a job. "Bob, I was wondering…" I wrinkle my nose with just a twinge of having a second thought about what I'm about to say.

"Yes?"

"The day that Officer Daniel arrested you, he asked you a question that you didn't answer."

Bob hangs his head. "Why did I take my puppies to Salem every day when I'm retired and don't need puppy care?"

I nod my head.

He rubs his temples. "It's true. I didn't really need Salem to watch the puppies. I lied and told her I was volunteering at the senior center and needed someone to keep an eye on the dogs. Then I'd piddle around town or play a round of golf. You saw me on the course a time or two, Richard."

"I did."

"Couldn't your grandson have watched the dogs?" Mom asks.

"Devin? No. I love him. Don't get me wrong, but he's made some poor choices in his young life. I wouldn't leave a goldfish under his care. I didn't need to play that much golf or run errands in town. The truth is that I lied to Salem because I needed an excuse to see her. I was torn up about her dumping me, and I couldn't think of any other plausible excuse to see her without her slamming the door in my face. She acted tough, but she loved those puppies. I know she did."

"What did you see in that woman, Bob?" asks Dad.

"Richard!"

"You're such a gentle soul…and well, Salem…" Dad continues.

"Bristled?" Bob asks, smiling.

"That's the perfect word choice."

"Salem was a hard nut to crack, but she and I had some lovely conversations about her life and her dreams. She doesn't…didn't…like to let people too close. I suppose that's why she was the love them and leave them type to most people. She could be quite fun. Just ask the gentlemen in this community." He shrugs his shoulders. "But once she realized that I really wanted to get to know *her* and not just the physical side, I really got to see the beauty of her soul."

"Huh," is all Mom can manage to say.

I suppose we may never fully understand Bob's attraction to Salem, but there is no denying that he had a strong one. There is no way he could have murdered Salem.

"Bob, do you think it's possible that Salem was counterfeiting books and selling them illegally online through her vintage book business?" I ask, watching him carefully.

"Counterfeit books?" He squints his eyes as if thinking hard about his answer. "I'm not sure. I suppose it's possible. I honestly never understood how she could afford her finer tastes with the money she brought in from that little bookstore. I didn't get involved with her business, though, at least not that kind of business," he chuckles. Every time Bob answers a question about Salem he smiles, a bright sparkle in his eyes as if imagining himself with her again for that moment in time. I hope someday to have someone in my life who loves me like he loved Salem.

Chapter 20

"Don't forget about karaoke tonight," says Mom as I grab my purse to run some errands, including getting a temporary covering of the lovely graffiti on my parents' car.

"I'll help you get Dad inside, but I really am not in the mood to do karaoke."

"Nonsense! Everyone is going to be there, Rosi. Please come. We'll grab dinner there. They have wonderful nachos in the bar."

"My dream. Bar nachos," I say as I smack my forehead.

"You're only here for another week. Everyone will be so disappointed if you don't come."

"Do you promise not to make me sing?"

"It's karaoke, Rosi. You *have to sing!*"

"Quit pestering her, Renee."

"Fine! You don't have to sing, but you might change your mind!" Mom's eyes are twinkling with so much joy right now she just might burst, like an overfilled water balloon attached to the hose.

"What time do you want to leave?"

"Be ready to go by 5:00!"

I sigh. "I'll be here." I grab my parents' car keys like I'm sixteen again. I take their car to Denny's Detailing on Front Street per Officer Kelly's recommendation. I'd called this morning, and they had promised to give the car a temporary fix until it can be permanently painted when my parents get back to Illinois.

I stop at the bakery in Tucson Valley first, the one right outside the entrance to the Tucson Valley Retirement Community. I choose two types of cupcakes, one vanilla with chocolate frosting and one chocolate with vanilla frosting. I overhear the woman at the counter ahead of me talking about a vandalism on Wild Cactus Drive. Oh, great, the gossip is spreading as fast as pee in a swimming pool.

"I hadn't heard," says the young clerk, clearly used to her gossipy shoppers and quite disinterested in their stories.

When the woman turns around, I know exactly who she is—Brenda with the overdone face and the white poodle named Ralphie who thinks he owns the sidewalk. I wish I'd brought Barley with me so she could bark at Ralphie from the car window.

"Rosi?" she says. "I haven't seen you in quite some time, since, I believe, you walked out on your mother's lovely brunch."

I smile until a new set of wrinkles form around my eyes. "Lovely to see you, Brenda. Please give Ralphie my love." I walk calmly to the car. But, after starting the car, I peel out of the gravel-covered parking lot, not caring a bit if I send a pebble flying through Brenda's windshield.

Before my appointment at the detailing shop, I use my GPS to find Miller Park where Keaton had told me his crew would be mulching the flower beds today. I'm regretting my purchase of the map of Southwest Arizona as I haven't ventured beyond Tucson Valley the entire time I've been here. I park next to a row of saguaro cacti along the street. Without the play structures, I'm not sure I could identify much of this land as a park. It's so dry and dirty compared to the lush green grass of a Midwest park, although I can spy Keaton and his team trying hard to build up a man-made berm at the far corner of the park with bags of black dirt, as yet unplanted flowers, and mulch. I didn't tell him I was coming to see him, and I don't want to make a scene in front of his co-workers. I decide to try to get his attention by casually walking along the south side of the park in hopes that he will look up at just the time I am passing by and happily, yet discretely, leave his co-workers and join me on the sidewalk where we can walk somewhere more private, and I can give him the cupcakes as a thank you for calming me in the middle of the night, well, at least keeping me company. But the universe has other plans for me. While looking at a purplish-colored hummingbird attracted to the colorful flowers of a blooming cactus, I trip over a small boulder outlining the public bathrooms by the toddler playground and land with my palms outstretched into a cactus shrub.

"Oww! Oww! Son of a…Oww! Oww!" I sit on the ground and begin picking cactus spines out of my hand, tears streaming down my face.

"Ma'am, are you okay?" I look up to see a man in khaki pants, a dirty shirt, and work gloves staring down at me. Right behind him are two other men, similarly dressed. And one of those men is Keaton.

"Rosi?"

"Hi!" I wave. "How's everyone today?"

"Well, we're doing a bit better than you," says Keaton. He looks at his co-workers. "I think I can take care of things from here, guys. Thanks. Why don't you take your lunch break a little early?"

When the men have gone back to their trucks, Keaton sits down on the ground next to me. He takes my right hand in his and pulls out three spines. "Let me see your other hand."

"I'm sorry I embarrassed you," I say, wishing I could evaporate.

"You didn't embarrass me, Rosi. Hey, look at me." He gently tips up my chin until I am forced to look into his milk chocolate eyes. "I was worried about you. No one should have to file a police report and fall into a cactus bush in the same day." A huge smile dances across his face.

I smile, too. It's so easy to grin at Keaton even when I am sitting next to a toddler-size playground with bleeding palms. "I got you something," I say, looking at the two plastic containers holding cupcakes that have been flipped upside down a foot in front of us.

Keaton picks up the containers. "You bought me cupcakes?"

I nod my head and shrug my shoulders. "I wanted to thank you for coming to my rescue last night. Now I need to get you something for removing cactus spines. Jazz hands!" I say, giggling uncomfortably at myself.

"You didn't need to buy me anything. It was my pleasure to help you last night. I'm really glad you called." He bends down close to my face. "And how did you know that smashed cupcakes were my favorite dessert?"

I chuckle softly. "I need to leave. I have an appointment at the detailer to get a temporary fix for my little problem." I point to my parents' car which is thankfully parked far enough away that his co-workers can't tease him about the girl with the graffiti car, too.

Keaton helps me up by the elbows. "Don't go yet. I've got a first-aid kit in my truck. Let's bandage those hands or you won't even be able to hold the steering wheel."

I follow Keaton to his truck. He pulls out two large bandages and antibacterial ointment from a tackle box in the back of his truck. I let him doctor my hands, so gently and assuredly. For the first time, I realize I am sad about having to leave in another week.

"All better!" Keaton smiles. "Why do you look so down? Are you in a lot of pain? Because I can give you some acetaminophen, too, if you want it. Let me check…"

I shake my head no. "I'm not in pain. Thanks again for your help."

"Are we still on for dinner tomorrow?"

"As long as we don't eat food where I need a fork and a knife at the same time."

"You are a silly young woman, Rosisophia Doroche."

I blush at the sound of my full name. "I am far from a *young* woman."

"Age is only a number. And you *are* young, at least compared to the women around here."

I roll my eyes.

"Plus, you are young at heart, full of adventure and *misadventure*." Keaton winks at me, and I think my heart flutters.

"Perhaps this trip has taught me that I need to embrace the craziness of life a bit more—lean in rather than out."

"That sounds awesome. May I lean in before you go?"

I look around to make sure his co-workers aren't watching and won't add to the razzing he's likely to get from my entry into Miller Park. When I don't see anyone, I shake my head yes. Keaton lays a firm kiss on my lips. I close my eyes and kiss him back. I'm not sure I recognize who I am anymore.

Chapter 21

I sit in the detailing shop waiting for the work on my parents' car to be completed. The shop said they could paint the driver's side panel a deep, navy blue color that would do a decent job of covering the graffiti until my parents get back to Illinois and have the dealership do an exact match. I try catching up on emails and text messages on my phone.

Thanks for the talk. Have a safe trip home.

I roll my eyes. Now that our business has settled and he's gotten what he perceives as a fair settlement when we sell the house, Wes is thoughtful enough to send a nice text. He doesn't deserve the right to wish me well on my trip home. He doesn't get the privilege of knowing where I am, when I'm away, if I'm safe. If he'd really cared, he wouldn't have brought Cara into our home and slept with her in our bed. I also have a text from Zak.

How is Grandpa? Set a new course record at the disc golf course in Lockport. Miss you.

I'm guessing that Wesley told Zak I'd finalized the outstanding matters of business. Sure, I was relieved they didn't turn me into the police after I made a poor decision in a momentary lapse into hysteria, but when he'd involved

Zak with our business, I'd been none too pleased. He hasn't told me he's missed me at all this winter. I haven't seen Zak since Christmas break, and yet now that his dad is pleased as punch with my *maturity* as he's phrased it, suddenly Zak is sentimental for his mother again. Why was *I* the bad guy to begin with? I didn't start this mess. I had plans of raising my family until they put me in the grave and threw roses on top of my casket. I didn't plan on being 39 and divorced and losing my job and losing the respect of my kid.

As I'm having a temporary pity party for myself, I look out toward the street of Tucson Valley. Something catches my attention—or someone. Across the street Officer Kelly is walking into the pawn shop. She's wearing jeans and a pink cardigan, not her police uniform. While police officers are certainly allowed a day off, I'd just seen Officer Kelly this morning and know that she is working today. If she needed to go into the pawn shop on official business, wouldn't she be wearing her uniform?

"Ma'am, your car is ready to go," says a young man who is wiping his hands on a dirty rag.

"Great. Thanks so much for getting us in so quickly."

"No problem. We couldn't' let you go driving around town with that kind of message plastered on your car now, could we?" He smiles in a most judgmental way, more of a smirk spreading across his face.

I choose to ignore the comment. "Can I pay now?" I watch Officer Kelly driving away in a car that is not her police cruiser. That was a quick trip.

"Sure. And you'll find your car parked out front."

"Thanks."

Before I drive back to my parents' house, I decide to visit the pawn shop across the street. A bell atop the door rings as I enter. No one comes out to greet me. I look around seeing a variety of items for sale: coins, tools, an electric skillet like Mom used to cook bacon on when I was a kid, video games I recognize from Zak's Xbox system, a violin, and many other items I have no use for.

"Can I help you?" A young woman with purple hair, large green glasses, and a tattoo arm sleeve leans over the counter with a giant smile on her face.

"Umm, hi, thanks. Maybe. I had a…friend…who may have been in here a short time ago, a young woman…"

"Morgan?"

"Yes, Morgan. She, um…told me about some items she saw that I might be interested in."

The young woman frowns. "That's odd. Morgan doesn't buy anything here. She just sells her jewelry."

"Oh, that's what I meant. She said I might be interested in some jewelry. Is it possible to see some of the jewelry she's sold you?"

"Sure. She's brought me some of the nicest pieces we've had since I've worked here. In fact, it's crazy, but you literally *just* missed her!" The woman walks to the end of the counter and waves her hand over the jewelry in the case in the counter. "She gave us those three necklaces on the top as well as those two rings. I haven't had a chance to price them yet. Sorry about that." She shows me a sapphire and diamond ring and a ring with a green stone that looks lighter than an emerald. Maybe a peridot?

"These are beautiful," I say, and I mean it, too. "My friend—*Morgan*—did mention that she had been bringing you some of her jewelry, but I can't remember which relative she said they'd belonged to."

"She never told me. She simply said that she'd recently been given some jewelry and that she wasn't really a fancy jewelry person herself. She said she's trying to make enough money to move her boyfriend to Arizona."

"Boyfriend? Yes, I remember that conversation, too. Would you mind if I took some pictures of this jewelry? I think my mother might be interested in a piece or two."

"Not at all. Go right ahead. I'll take them out of the case."

After I've snapped pictures of the jewelry, I thank the young woman, retrieve the car, and drive to the local library where I park in the shade. I pull out my phone to send a text.

Hi, Sparrow. This is Rosi Laruee. I wanted to give you an update on my visit to Salem's Stories. I didn't get a chance to do too much digging into Salem's computer because Barry arrived. After he went into Salem's office, I checked the computer screen where I found some emails from disgruntled patrons who'd purchased books they believed to be counterfeit, but I had to leave before he saw me—only I think he may have spotted me on a video recording later—but that's another story. I'm sending some pictures of jewelry that I found in the Tucson Valley Pawn Shop. Do these pieces look familiar? Thanks, Rosi

I send the pictures with the text message.

A few seconds later, my phone dings.

OMG! Those are Salem's rings and necklaces.

Chapter 22

Barley incessantly nips at my toes as I am getting ready to take my parents to karaoke at the Tucson Valley Senior Center. They'd apparently worked hard to get a permit to serve beer at their bar when they added the addition in 2015. It's the place to be on the third Saturday of the month I've been told. I've decided to wear black capris and a green and yellow tank top with a black sweater shrug. I let Barley continue to lick my toes as I put on a strappy pair of sandals. Sandals in February is a lovely thing. I put Barley's leash on when I am dressed and lead her through the house to the back door.

"You can leave her in the house," says Dad. "She will be more comfortable in here."

"Are you sure?"

"I'm sure. Just take her potty and let her back in."

"You're a softy."

"Maybe I am. She's a good girl, though. Aren't you a good dog, Barley?" He ruffles her fur and lets her lick him on the face.

"Enough of that!" says Mom who enters the room wearing a hot pink skirt and yellow leggings. Her shirt looks like the results from an explosion of neon paint, and her bangs rise high with enough hairspray to open the ozone layer.

Dad and I both stare at her with our mouths wide open. "What are you wearing?" I ask.

"I told you! You never listen to me, either of you! You are just alike! It's '80s theme night at the bar!"

"I thought you meant '80s music, not you-have-to-dress-like-Madonna night!" I say. Dad bursts into a fit of laughter which gets Barley excited. She starts running around the house and barking.

"You two are no fun!" says Mom, pouting. "Can't you change, Rosi?"

"No way, Mom. You're lucky I've even agreed to go to this thing."

"Fine. Richard, go change."

"Change?" he says from his recliner. "I've got on my tighty whities, a respectable pair of neutral-colored pants, a blue golfing shirt, and black socks. I'm as dressed as I'll be."

"No! You must wear the jean jacket and headband I have laid out in the bedroom."

"Those things? I thought you were making a donation pile for the resale shop. Now, if you mean my icy scarf, I can put *that* around my neck." An evil smile spreads across his face as he taunts my mother.

"Not funny. Go!" She points to the bedroom. Dad hangs his head and stomps with his cane every step he takes. But he goes.

I start the car and wait for my parents' argument to end. I receive a text from Sparrow.

Can you share your new information with Officer Daniel tomorrow? Thanks.

Great, just what I don't want to do—go see Officer Daniel—especially since I have to make an appointment so that Officer Kelly is not there.

Dad looks hysterical in his jean jacket and neon orange sweatband. Mom beams with pride as she sits in the backseat behind Dad. I'm kind of surprised that she didn't wear her Golden Girls t-shirt that was signed by Bea Arthur. "Are there prizes for best-dressed couple?" I ask.

"There sure are," says Mom, smiling from ear to ear. "And I think we have a real chance this year. I may have told a little fib, too." She giggles like a schoolgirl who is gossiping about a cute boy. "I told Jan and Brenda I was too busy with Richard's surgery and your visit to plan a couple's outfit. I can't wait to see the look of surprise on their faces when we stroll in looking like we walked right out of 1985."

"Yeah, that's exactly the vibe I get, too." Mom smacks the back of my seat.

The music is pumping loudly from the senior center as we walk toward the door. Dad has pulled the walker back out though he mostly uses the cane around the house. I don't think he and his walker will be making an appearance on the dance floor, however.

Brenda makes a beeline for Mom when she sees us walk in. "Renee Laruee, you nasty woman. You lied about your costumes!"

I laugh because I know exactly where the phrase *nasty woman* has come from. Mom does, too, and I know she doesn't appreciate the comment.

"Brenda, it's called a *surprise!*"

"Hmph! Fine. Follow me. We saved you seats at our table."

Mom makes a face behind Brenda's back. We follow Brenda to a table next to the dance floor. We can't possibly miss her as she's wearing a neon yellow spandex jumpsuit with bright orange leg warmers. Her legs look like toothpicks. It's hard to see past her Aqua-netted, bottle blonde hair. Jan and Frank are seated at the circular table near the dance floor. My face drops the moment I lay eyes on Jan and her overly done-up face because she doesn't take her eyes off me while tapping wildly on the arm of the man sitting next to her. I know instantly who the man with the tiny curls in his black hair and matching mustache must be—Allen, Jan's nephew. If Mom knew he'd be here tonight, she is in so much trouble. It's one thing to surprise her friends with '80s costumes. It's quite another to sabotage her own daughter with a setup with the man with the leather jacket, white t-shirt, and rolled-up jeans that I see when he stands up to make introductions. I mean, he's not even dressed for the right decade. It's '80s night. Duh!

As if reading my mind, Mom shakes her head *no* subtlety at both Dad and me because he is suspicious, too. "Renee! Richard! You sly dogs!" says Jan who taps Mom on the shoulder with her lace-gloved hand. Madonna she is *not*. "But, nonetheless, I think it is going to be hard to beat Madonna and Dick Tracy." She points to her husband Frank who is wearing Warren Beatty's classic yellow suit and yellow hat that he'd worn in the movie of the same name while dating Madonna. I have to stop myself from telling her she looks more like the current Madonna.

Dad's face says exactly what I am thinking. How could Mom be friends with these arrogant, rude women—at least Jan and Brenda? And then I see Karen, sitting quietly next to Jan's husband. She smiles and waves.

Paula reaches for my hand. It bristles from my cactus injuries. "It's lovely to see you again, Rosi."

I wonder what brought all of these women together and if some of them have to go together because they are related—like that sister-in-law you can't avoid because she comes with the family. The positive qualities in this group of women are not dispersed evenly amongst them. I make a mental note to ask Mom later.

"Rosi, please introduce yourself to my nephew Allen. This sweet boy surprised us by arriving a day early. He can change his schedule like that, you know, because he's the boss of his own company." She squeezes Allen's shoulder. He looks adoringly at his aunt.

They both turn their attention to me, waiting for me to introduce myself. I consider turning on the heels of my strappy sandals and walking back to the car. I feel someone tugging on the back of my cardigan. *Mom.* I take a deep breath before talking. "Hello, I'm Rosi. It's nice to meet you. Enjoy yourselves tonight. If you'd excuse me,

I'm going to get a drink." Then I turn around and walk to the bar. I can hear an audible gasp coming from Jan's mouth. It makes me smile.

"Is she always this rude?" I hear her say too loudly.

But my smile doesn't last long. "Let me get your drink. You go take a seat next to your parents." Allen brushes past me toward the bar before I can stop him. I return to the table and sink, defeated, into my chair.

"I'm so sorry," Mom whispers into my ear.

"Isn't Allen such a gentleman, Rosi?" asks Jan. "You two are going to have so much fun this week!"

"Leave the poor girl alone," says Dick Tracy, aka Frank.

"Somebody at this table could take a lesson or two from Allen," she says, getting up and walking to the karaoke table to put in her request, I presume. The setup is simple. A small karaoke machine sits on a long table with two microphones with long cords that are hooked into the machine.

"Has anyone heard anything new about Salem's case?" asks Brenda, her large record-shaped earrings dancing in the air as she speaks.

"I am sure the police will figure things out," says Karen. "We have a very low crime rate in Tucson Valley, and we want to keep it that way."

It's the most I've ever heard Karen speak. She certainly plays against type with a name like Karen. Poor woman. It's not her fault that her name was hijacked to indicate crabby, entitled women making a scene. Jan and Brenda are more Karen than Karen.

"I hope you are right, Karen," says Paula. "It's scary to think that someone could be murdered in our shopping district. What if it was a robbery or something like that? Why, any one of us could have been shopping downtown and been at the wrong place at the wrong time. Maybe that's what happened to poor Salem." Paula is wearing a jean skirt and a brown George Straight t-shirt. Her short hair features a large barrette shaped like a butterfly. She looks like she's just come from Cowboy Donnie's church service.

"No way. This was a targeted murder," says Jan. "Salem made somebody really mad. She probably overstepped her bounds with the wrong husband."

"Are you suggesting that somebody's *wife* killed Salem?" asks Brenda, her eyes getting large.

"All I am saying is that it's possible. Lord knows that woman tried getting her claws into many a man in this retirement community," says Jan.

"But she never made any moves on any of *our* husbands, though, right?" asks Paula whose pasty-skinned husband looks sickly sitting next to her.

"I always thought that was odd," says Jan.

Someone kicks me under the table. I don't dare look at Mom. I know the sacrifice she made to protect her friends from Salem's wandering eyes getting too close to their husbands. And her guilty conscience for helping Salem to buy counterfeiting supplies in exchange for this protection will go to the grave with us.

"Here you go, my lady."

Allen hands me a glass of wine. He didn't even ask me what I wanted to drink. I'm not 21. I have an opinion when it comes to my alcohol of choice. I have an acquired taste for specific drinks, but I suppose a white wine is better than red. At least Allen got that one right. "Thank you."

Jan returns to the table after putting in her karaoke request just as Allen is about to take the empty seat on the other side of Frank. "No, Allen. Frank, move over. Let Allen have your seat."

Frank sighs and shifts over a chair, letting Allen have the chair next to me. Why did I agree to come here tonight?

"Let me order some appetizers for the table!" Mom says, jumping up so fast that she nearly knocks over my glass of wine.

Dad slides over to Mom's chair so that he is on the other side of me. He whispers in my ear. "Rosi, your mom told me she had no idea, but Jan can be a real witch to her when she doesn't get her way. I know it's not fair to ask, but if you could humor *Jan* just until the costume awards are announced, I know how grateful Mom would be."

Dad's eyes are pleading earnestly. How can I say no to my dad when he's being so sweet? And I know how tormented Mom is right now. She was protecting her friends when she agreed to help Salem. Who knows why she'd want to protect someone like Jan or Brenda, but she does. I remind myself that no one knows me here in my authentic life besides my parents, so if I need to put on a metaphorical mask and pretend to have fun for a couple of hours to protect my mother's standing in this retirement community, then I guess I can do that.

"And now, can I please have the lovely couple up here who requested 'Islands in the Stream' by Kenny Rogers and Dolly Parton?" Troy Kettleman is operating the karaoke machine. I wonder if that's part of the job description for the Tucson Valley mayor.

"That's you!" Jan says, looking at Allen. "And you, too, Rosi! Go on you two, young'uns!"

It's been a long time since I've been referred to as a "young'un." I look at Dad who smiles coaxingly. I close my eyes and sigh.

"Shall we, Dolly?" asks Allen. I swear his mustache twitches from side to side as he talks.

"Sure," I relent. I follow Allen with his leather jacket and rolled-up jeans to the table where the karaoke machine sits, the first line of the song prepped and ready to go. I notice that I am the same height as Allen. The words to "Islands in the Stream" appear on the screen.

"You sing Dolly's lines," Captain Obvious tells me.

I'm not a great singer, but I'm not terrible. Allen is a good singer, but not great. I look out into the crowd of people. An old man with bellbottoms—can't these people get their decades straight—is dancing with his wife who is in a wheelchair. He is rolling her back and forth, stopping to walk around her chair. Every time he passes in front of her, he kisses her on the cheek. It's about the sweetest thing I have ever seen. I decide to let loose on the last chorus, giving it everything I have in me. I can pretend for a little longer. Allen smiles and nods his head, encouraging me. I am thinking that I am killing it because the crowd is clapping like crazy, but then I notice the laughter rising from the crowd. It takes me a second to realize why they are laughing. Allen is pointing his finger at my breasts and shaking his head side to side enthusiastically as if to say, *she doesn't have what Dolly has.* I am mortified. How dare this stranger humiliate me for kicks? Sorry, Dad, but I can't pretend anymore. I throw my microphone on the ground. It makes a screeching noise because it's too close to the speaker, and the same people who had been laughing at me are now throwing their hands over their ears, even the sweet lady in the wheelchair. She hadn't been laughing, though. I stomp across the dance floor to the far end of the bar. I know I can't leave my parents here, but they can't make me go back to their table, either.

"Can I have a vodka tonic?" I ask the bartender whose back is to me. How else am I going to make it through the rest of this night?

"That's quite a strong drink, isn't it, young lady?"

I snap my head up at the sound of the familiar voice. "Keaton?"

"Alex P. Keaton tonight, Rosisophia Doroche," he whispers. "It is our night—'80s kids and all—right?"

"What are you doing here?"

"I bartend on the side—a man of many talents. He grins. How's your hand?"

His smile is the nicest thing I have seen all night. I open the palms of my hands where the tiniest of pinpricks remain from my run-in with the cactus earlier today. "I'm good. Thanks." I look toward the karaoke machine where an old man is singing "Beat It" by Michael Jackson. "You didn't…you didn't see…?"

"I most certainly did. You've got some pipes, Rosi. But who's the snake that was singing with you?"

I drop my head onto the bar, full of embarrassment.

"Hey! Stop it. He's the one that looked like an idiot, not you."

"Then why was the crowd laughing along with him?"

"They're a bunch of idiots, too. Here's your vodka tonic. Drink up—assuming your mother can drive you home."

"She will. She owes me big time."

I stay at the bar eating peanuts out of the shells while Keaton works the crowd at the bar. He's very endearing to the old women whom he serves.

"Hey, I have a break coming up. How about we sing a new duet? Make them forget about that idiot?"

"You can't be serious," I say.

"I'm as serious as a heart attack!"

"Don't say that too loudly around here. Yikes! *If* I were to agree, what song do you have in mind for my encore?"

"I've Had the Time of My Life," says Keaton easily.

"From *Dirty Dancing*?" I ask surprised. "Uh, and I suppose you're going to suggest that I fly into your arms, so you can hoist me by the waist above your head for all to see?"

"Well, maybe we'll skip the running bit without practice, but I think I can lift you in the air and do a little spin around. That should be enough to get *this* crowd excited."

"You can't lift me up," I say dryly.

"I most certainly can." Keaton flexes his arms.

"I'm no spring chicken."

"What does that even mean? You are adorably fit. I'm the one who's in his 40s! Come on, let's practice." Keaton yells to the other bartender that he's going on break, and I follow him out a back door marked *employees only* and into an empty hallway. "Okay, let's practice. Do you mind it I grab you by the waist?"

I can feel my face flush, and I wish I'd worn a higher necked tank so my chest didn't glow red, too. I nod my head yes. Keaton puts his hands onto each side of my waist. I collapse in a fit of laughter the minute he touches my hips. "I'm sorry! I'm very ticklish."

"Let's try again."

The same thing happens as I bend at the waist upon his touch. I'm laughing so hard that a stream of air escapes from behind. Now, any chance of pulling myself together is over.

"Did you just fart?" Keaton asks, a twinkle in his eyes.

My sides ache from laughing, and I don't care anymore. "I did. It was me. I own it." I raise my hand in the air as a sign of admittance.

"Huh. There's a first time for everything. Come on. You're hopeless. We have a duet to sing."

"You're not going to lift me, though, right?"

He winks at me. "Just be ready for anything."

"Oh, and you know I'm not a great singer, right?" I ask as I follow him back into the bar.

"I've heard!" he laughs. Keaton walks confidently to Troy Kettleman. He whispers in his ear.

I look at my parents' table. Everyone seems lost in deep conversation, probably gossiping. The lovely man who'd danced with his wife in the wheelchair is helping her with a drink of water. Allen is dancing with Brenda to a man's rendition of a-ha's "Take on Me." He's spinning her around the dance floor so much I think she might flop over. He's certainly earning points with the old ladies in the audience. Guys like that are all show with no substance.

When the a-ha wannabe is done singing, Keaton beckons me to him with his finger. I brush past Allen without a look though I can see him through my peripheral vision when he turns his head to look at me. The music to

"I've Had the Time of My Life" starts playing. Keaton and I sing the words on the screen. I haven't sung this song since I listened to the '80s station on the radio in my car when I drove to and from my first job at a small town newspaper, but it comes back to me easily. Keaton is a showman, really getting into Bill Medley's part. As we near the end of the song when Patrick Swayze lifts Jennifer Grey in the air, I tighten my stomach and take a step to the side. Keaton can't lift me if he can't reach me. But he steps over, too. He glances at me. My eyes widen in surprise, and before I can stop what is happening, Keaton lifts me from behind and holds me up in the air as if he is Rafiki holding up the baby cub Simba for all the senior center members to ooh and ahh over. When he puts me back on the ground, the crowd erupts in applause. Keaton and I join our hands together, raising them in the air, and taking a bow in the center of the dance floor. I am so out of breath I can barely speak. I have also peed my pants—a little. It's what happens when you've given birth to a ten-pound baby.

"Thanks for not farting in my face again," Keaton says.

I elbow him in the ribs. "And thanks for not dropping me!" I decide to keep my incontinence to myself.

The last thing I need is for people to say, *Hey, that's the girl who peed down her leg!* every time they see me. It's not *that* bad yet.

"I could have held you up there for another five minutes!" Keaton flexes as I follow him off the dance floor. "That was fun." He looks at the crowd who is still clapping. "I have to get back to the bar, Rosi."

"I know. Thanks for helping me to reclaim my pride."

"Anytime." He leans down and kisses me on the lips before walking back behind the bar. "I'll pick you up at 7:00 tomorrow night for that proper date."

I am still smiling when I return to my parents' table after tidying up in the bathroom. Everyone gives me another round of applause—except for Jan and Allen.

"Rosi, that was wonderful! When did you and Keaton learn that song?" asks Mom gleefully. "And *that lift?* That was fantastic!"

"You put a smile on this old man's face," says Dad. "That makes this whole night worth it." He kisses me on the cheek when I sit down.

"We practiced for about five minutes in the employee hallway. It wasn't exactly what we'd planned, but it was fun."

"Don't you think she was wonderful?" Mom trolls Jan.

"Sure, if you like that showmanship kind of thing," she says.

"The singing was fine," I guess, says Brenda. That is one tight grump-supports-grump friendship.

"I thought our duet was better," says Allen, patting me on the top of my hand that sits on the table. He then squeezes my hand and doesn't remove it until I shake it free.

"And now the time you've all been waiting for," says Troy Kettleman. He stands in the middle of the dance floor with a microphone in one hand and a trophy in the other. The rhinestones on his cowboy boots twinkle under the neon strobe lights. "I'd like to ask all of those couples here tonight who are dressed in our '80s theme to come to the dance floor, please." Mom, Dad, Jan, Frank, Brenda and Paula with their husbands, and at least ten other couples walk to the dance floor. Troy beams a bit unnaturally at the couples, and I wonder if he's thinking about Salem and wishing he were part of an '80s themed dance couple with her right now. I wonder if she'd even come to an event like this. It's kind of cruel to leave out the single people in this competition. I imagine there are many widowers or divorcees here in costume, too, like Karen.

Troy looks at the couples dressed before him in an alluring display of teased hair, neon colors, and legwarmers. "The senior center board has voted, and the best dressed couple, according to theme is…" Troy puts his hand over his face and rubs his chin. "The best dressed couple is…" He closes his eyes and blinks them several times. Is he crying? "I'm sorry, I…"

A woman with shoulder pads in her yellow jacket takes the microphone from Troy. "It's okay, Troy. Thank you. Ladies and gentlemen, the trophy for the best dressed couple goes to Richard and Renee Laruee!"

"Yeah!" I jump up from my seat like a little girl, clapping my hands in glee. Jan looks shocked, but I'm not going to be the one to tell her that Warren Beatty and Madonna dated in the '90s, not the '80s.

Mom hugs Dad. She retrieves the trophy and holds it high above her head. I watch Troy Kettleman walk past the bar and out of the senior center. He must really miss Salem. It seems Bob and Troy are *both* mourning her hard.

"Did you know that I am CEO of the largest rat extermination company in Washoe County, Nevada, Rosi?"

I had forgotten that Allen was still sitting at the table. "I had no idea, Allen. That's really something, isn't it?"

"It really is," he says, clearly not recognizing sarcasm.

When Dad has safely collapsed into his recliner after we get home, I let Barley into the house after her potty break. She jumps on my lap. Mom doesn't even shoo her off the couch.

"What was wrong with Troy tonight?" asks Dad as he reaches over his chair and pets Barley on the top of her head.

"I don't know. Maybe he was thinking about Salem while he was standing on the dance floor with all of those couples around him," Mom says. She sets her trophy on the fireplace mantel though I can't imagine for the life of me why anyone in Tucson needs a fireplace.

"I sure wish I knew if there was going to be an arrest soon for her murder. It's maddening to think that a murderer might still be free in Tucson Valley.

I groan. "Sparrow asked me to pass along a message to Officer Daniel tomorrow. I'll let you know if I find out anything new. I'm going to get ready for bed now." Barley jumps off the couch to follow me into the bathroom.

"Rosi?"

"Yes, Mom?"

She sits on the edge of Dad's recliner looking ten years younger tonight with her bright-colored makeup, especially when she smiles. "You don't have to go on a pickleball date with Allen."

"I wasn't planning to. But thanks for your permission," I smirk.

"Yeah, he's a tiny little worm."

I can't stop laughing, and it feels so good to laugh.

Chapter 23

On my morning walk with Barley, I find myself walking toward Bob's home again. I tell myself it's just a desire to let Barley see her mama, but I know it's really because I want to check on Bob. The only family I've seen with him these last couple of weeks is a less-than-empathetic-seeming grandson.

The sun is shining in my eyes as I turn the corner onto Bob's block. That's why I don't see the family of javelinas, two adults and two babies, walking in my direction until they cross my path on the sidewalk. Barley growls and barks at the boar-like beasts who dare get too close. They aren't interested in spending any more time with us than we want to spend with them, but I'm rattled. I watch them cross between two homes across the street, shuddering involuntarily as their little hooves patter on the pavement. I'm glad my parents have a fenced-in backyard.

"You should have seen the look on your face," I hear from someone walking toward me with a dog. It's Devin and Suzi.

"Good morning, Devin. I imagine it was a look of sheer terror."

He laughs. "It was."

"Are there a lot of javelinas in the neighborhood?" Suzi and Barley smell each other while we talk on the sidewalk.

"I've never seen more than four at a time, but Grandpa says he thinks there might be forty or fifty wild javelinas in and around the retirement community."

"Yikes! They're just like deer back home, I guess."

"Do deer run down sidewalks in neighborhoods?" He wrinkles his forehead in confusion.

"Fair point." I hesitate for a second, and he tugs at Suzi to continue their walk. "Devin, wait a minute. I'd like to ask you a question."

"Yeah?"

I never minded Zak's teenage years. He was amenable most of the time. Devin, however, fits the stereotype of an entitled, spoiled, disinterested teenager. I choose my words carefully. "Are you and Barry Mansfield friendly?" I already know the answer, but I am trying to gauge his reaction.

"Why?"

"I've...I've heard some rumors about some illegal activities he may be a part of, and I...I...want to make sure you are aware that there are people who know about this."

I stay as vague as possible. A little installation of fear in a sixteen-year-old can be a good thing.

"I told him he was stupid," he says, kicking a rock into the street. Suzi tries to chase it, but he pulls her back by the leash.

"What do you mean?"

"Look, nothing was my idea. Sure, he gave me some money, but I didn't ask for it. I just wanted to buy the new PS5 because Grandpa wouldn't give me money for one. He's so old-fashioned he actually wanted me to read a book. Can you *believe* that?"

This is proving to be easier than I'd imagined. "Why did Barry give you money, Devin?"

Devin looks from side to side as if there are people standing out on their rock-covered lawns on a Sunday morning waiting to get their next piece of gossip. "He told me he'd give me some money if I could pick the lock into his mom's bookstore. I might have some knowledge about how to do that. I'm not proud." He holds up his hands as if to virtually distance himself from his poor choices.

I can relate to poor choices, and I feel sorry for this boy. "Barry didn't have a key to Salem's Stories?"

"Not anymore. He said his mom took away his key when he found out about the…some…*stuff* she was doing in the store and threatened to tell her secrets. That ticked her off. She gave him a bunch of money to go away and then pretty much cut him out of her life, kind of like my parents did after I got arrested for shoplifting at Walmart." He hangs his head.

"Did your grandpa ever mention this *stuff* that Salem might have been doing?"

"Grandpa Bob?" He shakes his head from left to right adamantly. "No way. He didn't know anything. He was just stupidly blinded by whatever spell Salem cast on him."

"You've been really helpful, Devin. I think it might be best to stay away from Barry for a while."

"Don't worry. I got my PS5 money after I got him into the store. He paid me that same day in Salem's office and then kicked me out. I hope I don't ever have to see him again. He's not a very nice man. And he said a lot of awful things about his mom. I know my parents are disappointed in me right now, but I'd never call my mom the names he called his mom."

I ponder the boy before me, right on the cusp of manhood. "I know you probably don't want some stranger giving you advice, Devin, but I think maybe you should talk to your mom and dad. Your whole life is waiting for you. I think you've got a lot of good things in your future."

"Huh," is all he says. He tugs on Suzi's leash, and they continue down the sidewalk. But before he is out of view, Devin turns around and yells something to me.

"What?"

"Thanks! I just wanted to say thanks!"

I nod my head, tug on Barley's leash, and continue our walk, one more piece of the puzzle complete.

"And also!"

I have to strain to hear him. "Yes?"

"It was Barry who spray-painted your car!"

Now it's my turn to tell *him* thanks. And make those *two pieces* of the puzzle complete.

Chapter 24

When I'd called Officer Daniel at the station this morning, I'd asked for a private meeting. He hadn't questioned this request, and I believe he fancied that I'm interested in more than just a business meeting since I'd asked to meet at the coffee shop in the Mabel Brown Sports Complex in the retirement community. The truth is that I needed a place to meet where Officer Kelly would unlikely be patrolling.

Officer Daniel walks with confidence to my table in the back of the coffee shop, his self-importance on display, removing his hat, and tucking it under his arm pit as he approaches. "Good morning, Rosi." He nods his head but doesn't smile.

"Good morning. Thank you for agreeing to meet with me."

He sets his hat on the chair next to him and sits down. "I had to move some things around on my calendar—I'm a very busy man, you know—but I assumed this must be important."

I force a fake smile. "I am sure you must be quite busy. I imagine that Salem's murder has greatly increased your workload."

"You'd be correct. There hasn't been a murder on my watch until Ms. Mansfield. I pride myself in enforcing the law in Tucson Valley. We have a fine reputation as a wonderful place to live for the young *and* the old. My office has been working overtime to get this mystery solved. What brings me here, Rosi? If you are going to argue for Bob's innocence again, it's a waste of time. Every housewife and golfing buddy in Tucson Valley has vouched for Bob's character."

"No, that's not why…that's great, though. Bob *is* a good person, it seems. I have three matters I'd like to speak to you about. One, my parents know that I am no longer working with the Springfield Gazette, so your bribery for information is…"

Officer Daniel puts his hand on top of mine but only for a second. "I'm sorry. That was a rude thing for me to ask you to do."

I am caught off guard by his change in demeanor, and it makes me suspicious.

"I've never had a murder investigation in my jurisdiction. It's making me a little desperate for leads."

I sigh. "Then I might be able to shed some light on another theory—or two."

Officer Daniel puts his elbows on the table and leans forward. "Go on."

"Would you like coffee, Officer Daniel?" asks the waitress who deposits my coffee order on the table in front of me—black with two sugars. Stray pieces of hair hang out from her messy blonde bun, and she's wearing a low-cut, green V-neck shirt.

Officer Daniel shows off his smarmy grin and reminds me of his true nature. "Hello, Samantha. I'd love a coffee—black, *no sugar*," he emphasizes as if ordering a coffee with no sugar makes him morally superior.

When she has gone back to the kitchen for his coffee, I tell him about Sparrow giving me permission to enter Salem's Stories.

"Rosi! You had no right to go into that store. It was a crime scene." His eyes are blazing mad.

"Exactly. It *was* a crime scene. It's not anymore. How is my going in there any different than if Sparrow and Tina had gone in there?"

He doesn't have an answer. Instead, he sips his coffee which Samantha has delivered with a chocolate croissant—on the house.

"Anyway, while I was retracing my steps when I'd found Salem's body, the door opened." I'd already decided to keep Devin's appearance at Salem's Stories that day to myself. That kid doesn't need any more trouble.

"Didn't you lock it behind you?"

"Of course."

"Who else had a key?" Officer Daniel pauses midbite, awaiting my answer with interest.

"Barry."

"Salem's son? I didn't think they had much of a relationship from my interviews with Sparrow."

"I'm not sure what their *personal* relationship may have been, but I think they had a *working* relationship. Or perhaps Barry continued Salem's work after she died." I don't stop talking as he raises his eyebrows. "I watched Barry read something on the desktop computer behind the counter at the front of the store. After he went to the office, I ran to the computer and read a couple of emails. I took pictures with my phone if you want to see them." I hold out my phone as Officer Daniel reads the messages from James Nottingham and Nanette Collins that express their displeasure with being duped into buying counterfeit, vintage books.

Officer Daniel's mouth gapes open wide. "Wow. We took Ms. Mansfield's laptop for processing, but Officer Kelly ran a check on the desktop computer and said it was pretty dull stuff, just routine business transactions—nothing-to-see-here type of evidence."

"Oh, well, that's interesting to hear because that brings me to the third reason I brought you here today," I say as I take a sip of my coffee.

"My charm and good looks?" Officer Daniel raises his eyebrows at me across the table.

I spit out my coffee, sending it flying across the table and onto Officer Daniel's sparkling lieutenant badge. "I'm so sorry!" I have to try very hard not to smile as he's dabbing it dry with his napkin. I take a deep breath and continue. "It has come to my attention that a jewelry box belonging to Salem also went missing."

"How do you know all of this information?"

I shrug my shoulders. "I guess I was at the right place at the right time. I was getting my parents' car temporarily painted after the graffiti incident."

"What graffiti incident?" Officer Daniel pounds the table. "How come I don't know what is happening in my own jurisdiction?"

I am beginning to understand why nothing is moving forward with Salem's case. "Officer Kelly took my statement. My parents' car, which I've been using, was spray-painted with the words *Stop Snooping*. She took a full report. Haven't you seen it?" He doesn't answer. "Anyway—" I continue, exasperated with his incompetence, "as I was sitting in the detailing shop waiting on that temporary paint job, I saw Officer Kelly go into the pawn shop across the street."

"The Tucson Valley Pawn Shop?"

"Yes, are there other pawn shops in Tucson Valley?"

Officer Daniel ignores my question.

"I thought it was odd that she was wearing her day clothes and not her uniform. Seeing as I knew that it was a workday because she'd taken my statement in the morning—in her uniform—I was curious. So, after the car was finished, I walked across the street. And long story short, I found some jewelry there that the employee said she bought from Officer Kelly. I took pictures of the jewelry and sent them to Sparrow. She confirmed that the jewelry had come from Salem's missing jewelry box." I take a long sip of my coffee which the waitress has refreshed and sit back, exhausted from the mental gymnastics my mind has been doing trying to figure out the meaning of all this information again as I spoke it out loud to Officer Daniel.

Officer Daniel waves the waitress over to refill his third cup of coffee. This time he doesn't even have a flirty smile for her. "She really had the community fooled."

"What do you mean?"

"Who smiles that much on the job? It was all fake. But what I don't understand is *why* Morgan had Salem's jewelry. And did she know about those emails?"

"I guess that's something you are going to have to figure out."

"And I think I need to pay another visit to Salem's Stories. Do you still have that key?"

"I do."

"Let me talk to Ms. Mansfield's sister, and maybe...maybe you can come with me to the bookstore?"

I raise my eyes in surprise. "I'd like that."

Chapter 25

"How'd it go?" asks Mom. She is sitting on the couch with Barley curled up in her lap. She's graduated from the backyard to my bedroom to the couch to the lap rather quickly.

"Fine, I guess. He's going to take me with him back to Salem's Stories after he gets permission from Sparrow."

"Whatever for?"

"I'm not sure. Maybe he knows he can't rely on his partner anymore, and he wants a second set of eyes."

"Or he needed another excuse to see you," Dad laughs as he walks into the room. Today he's trying the "use the wall" approach to walking around the house.

"He knows there's no chance," I laugh.

"What about that landscaper?" Mom asks, raising her eyebrows.

"Keaton? He's fun, Mom. We have fun together, but I'm going back to Illinois soon. Long distance dating is not my cup of tea."

"Why do you have to go back next week, Rosi?" asks Dad.

"I think you are getting along fine without me. I'm sure you'd like to reclaim the second bedroom as your office so you can set your amateur radio equipment back up."

"I don't mind hijacking your mom's vanity in our bedroom for my equipment a bit longer if it means you'll stay."

"I need to find a job, Dad. I can't keep putting that off."

Barley jumps off the couch and barks at me. "I think this little girl wants a walk."

"When you get back, will you do me a favor?" Mom asks a little too sweetly than usual.

"I am *not* playing pickleball with Allen," I say through gritted teeth.

"Of course not. I wouldn't make you do that, Rosi," she pauses. "However, Karen cancelled as my partner today because she has a bunion on her foot. I was wondering if you'd consider playing with *me?*"

"I've never played pickleball in my life."

"I know, but it's an easy game to pick up."

"Why do you think all these old people play it so much?" Dad laughs.

Mom swats him with the closest AARP magazine. "Please, Rosi?"

I sigh. "Fine. I'll play, but I can't promise that I will be at your skill level. I haven't even picked up a tennis racket in at least a decade since Zak took lessons in elementary school."

"Perfect! Thank you. I'll get ready." She kisses me on the cheek before heading to her bedroom.

"I'm taking Barley for a quick walk!" I shut the door behind us and wonder what I've just gotten myself into.

The pickleball courts are outside the Mabel Brown Sports Complex where I'd met with Officer Daniel this morning. There are ten courts, all currently occupied by peppered or gray-haired men and women hitting a plastic ball a touch bigger than a tennis ball back and forth over a net with paddles (not *rackets* as Mom had informed me). Mom is wearing a black tennis skirt, the kind that looks like a skirt but is really a pair of shorts so you can still reach ungracefully for the ball, I guess, and not show all of your lady parts to your opponents. I've put my hair into a ponytail and dressed in Nike shorts and a lime green tank top and Adidas athletic shoes.

"Let's paddle up, shall we?"

"Paddle up?"

"Yep. I have sooo much to teach you! Put your paddle there." Mom points to a rack. She slides her paddle in, and I add mine next to hers. "Our paddles will advance to the left. It will be our turn to play on an open court when our paddles move all of the way to the left. Isn't that fun? That way, we don't ever have to worry about our competition. If we wanted to pick our competition, then we'd simply have our partners slot their paddles next to ours and we'd all move to an open court. But, since we don't care who we play today, the team next to us will be our competition. Got it?"

"I understand. Ingenious." She doesn't see me roll my eyes behind her back, not because I think the system is flawed but because I'm watching the teams on the court right now, and I am dreading agreeing to play with Mom because there are a lot of talented players in the Tucson Valley Retirement Community.

Jan and Frank lob and volley the pickleball as if the life of their grandchild were on the line. They don't miss a single ball the whole time I am watching. Their opponents, who look to be at least ten years older, have a hard time keeping up. I feel sorry for them. I also hope they bow out soon, or someone is going to break something. At least it's easy to pick up how the game is scored watching Jan and Frank rack up points.

"It's our turn, Rosi!" Mom picks up our paddles.

"Who are we playing?" I ask, though I only know a handful of people in the community. I am relieved that Jan and Frank are occupied.

"Fancy seeing you here."

I turn around to see Allen walking in the same direction as Mom. And following him is Brenda, who looks like she's had a fresh injection in her lips since karaoke night.

"Sorry," Mom whispers in my ear. "It was all chance."

If that's true, then the universe must be conspiring against me. "Hello, Allen. Brenda, so nice to see you again, too." Kill them with kindness. I mean, confuse them with kindness. Oh screw it, kill them with kindness!

"I didn't think I'd see the great Rosi Laruee on a pickleball court. I thought you might have pulled something when that cad picked you up the other night."

"Which side?" I ask Mom, ignoring Allen completely.

"Good one," I hear Brenda say to Allen behind my back.

Mom points out the lines on the court, giving me another refresher on the rules though she'd already covered everything in the car. No amount of reviewing will make me an effective pickleball player my first game. Mom serves first. She's got some moves. Brenda isn't ready, too busy adjusting her skintight tank top. Allen returns her next serve with ease, though, and the game kind of goes downhill from there.

"Good shot, Allen! Great swing, Brenda!" Jan cheers from the sidelines. Frank throws in a compliment for Mom every once in a while, which is appreciated, but there aren't too many good things to say about my play. Allen hits a shot deep in the court. As I'm reaching for the ball my left shoe trips over my right shoe, and I splay onto the court hard. Finesse has never been an adjective used to describe anything I've ever done.

"Are you okay?" asks Mom, dropping her paddle as she comes to check on me.

"You need a real teacher, Rosi. Are you sure you don't want Allen to give you a few tips?" Jan stares at me, daring me to sass her back.

The words are sitting on the tip of my tongue ready to spew my vitriol out at these women and her nephew, but I look at Mom's pleading eyes and close my mouth. Allen reaches out his hand. I take it. "Thanks." I brush off my pride and pick up my paddle.

"We can put you out of your misery. We accept your forfeit."

"We aren't forfeiting. We may not win, but we won't quit."

Allen shrugs his shoulders. "Suit yourself."

We lose the game 11-3. It's a humiliating defeat. I'm proud of my mom. She played so hard, trying to make up for my ineptitude. The process of moving and striking the ball at the same time proved quite challenging, especially since my hand is still healing from the cactus spines. Mom has flourished in this community, trying things she never did before in Illinois. She has made friends (some questionable) and tried activities that make her happy. She and Dad made the right decision to winter in Tucson Valley. Watching my mom thrive in this foreign environment was worth the humiliation of defeat.

We shake hands as good sports do after a game. Allen doesn't let go of my hand, though, until I pull it away forcefully.

I haven't sweat this much since last fall when Zak indulged me by going to a farm to pick out pumpkins. It was a rare warm fall day, and I'd picked too many pumpkins and gourds. The wagon I was dragging through the field lost a tire, and we had to carry our purchases the rest of the way to our car. I'd been reminded to stop setting such high expectations for mother/son moments, but when your kid only comes home for visits now and then, the opportunities to make memories take on more importance.

"I'm going to buy a seltzer water in the sports center. Want anything?" asks Mom.

"I'm good. Thanks. I'll meet you at the car. I'll take your paddle." She walks toward the sports center while I fumble for the key fob.

"I'm leaving tomorrow, Rosi."

I jump a little, startled by Allen's presence. I thought I was walking to my car alone, but I'm being followed closely by Allen and Brenda.

"Let me take you to dinner tonight. I'll give you some pointers that might improve your game." I think I see

Brenda pouting behind his back when Allen asks me out, but it might just be because she has massive lips.

"Allen, I am going to pass. I have plans tonight."

"Don't tell me you have plans with that *landscaper*." He says the word as if it's the most disgusting thing in the world.

Brenda falls into step with Allen, brushing her arm against his every chance she gets. There has to be a thirty-year age difference between them. Plus, Brenda is married. "Did you know that Allen is the CEO of his own company?" she gushes.

"I've heard." Why did we have to park so far away from the paddleball courts?

"Someone like you needs to be with an educated man," says Allen.

I turn around in the middle of the parking lot and glare at Allen. "And what makes you think that Keaton isn't educated?"

"He plays with dirt, Rosi," says Brenda.

"She has a point."

"And you kill rats, Allen. "Do you really hold yourself as morally superior?"

215

"You do *what?*" Brenda stands next to her Mercedes with her hands on her hips and her expression as pronounced as possible on her face.

Allen throws up his hands. "*I* don't kill the rats. I'm the CEO. It's a lucrative business."

"I can't believe Jan left out that little detail. Yuck!" Brenda gets into her car, slams her door, and drives away.

Allen's face betrays his frustration. "People like that beg for my time when there's a rat's nest in their attic."

"And I hope that if you ever need a landscaper, they're all booked, your grass dries up, and your flowers die!"

I get into the car to wait for Mom while Allen stands open-mouthed in the middle of the parking lot.

Chapter 26

Barley is banished to the backyard. I'm wearing a black dress with spaghetti straps for my dinner date with Keaton. I don't need dog hair as an accessory. I use a hair clip to hold the sides of my hair in place at the back of my head. A soft pink lipstick and light eyeliner and mascara are the final touches to my preparation. I haven't worn this much makeup all winter, especially without having an office to go into every day. I really need to find a new job as soon as I get home.

"Rosi, you look so pretty," says Mom who is sitting next to Dad in her matching recliner.

"My pretty girl," says Dad.

"Geesh, you guys act like I'm going to Prom."

"Those were fun days," Mom says wistfully.

"Do you not remember my senior Prom date?"

"Ian?"

"Yes, Ian who murdered his ex-wife when he caught her cheating."

"Oh my! I'd forgotten about that!"

"It sure makes a little tire slashing seem tame, doesn't it?" Dad smiles.

"Dad!"

"Richard!"

"What?" Dad throws his hands up in defense. "I'm just speaking the truth."

"You are incorrigible!" we say at the same time.

"Rosi, I'm sorry I judged Keaton unfairly. That was rotten of me to buy into rumors. He's a wonderful man."

"Thanks, Mom. You're forgiven." The doorbell rings.

"I'll get it," I say, walking in front of Mom who is reaching for the doorknob.

"Aren't you going to invite Keaton inside?" She looks like Barley when she knows we are about to leave, her sad eyes begging for attention.

"I am not. I am not a child and don't need my parents' permission. Don't wait up. And I love you!" I open the door and close it in quick succession before she can protest.

"Rosi! You startled me!"

"Don't tell me you are disappointed to not speak with my parents."

"Well, it *is* polite, no?"

"I am almost forty. I don't need my dinner companion to speak with my parents before dinner."

"Are you okay?" Keaton stares at me for a moment too long, and I feel the panic coming. "I'm sorry. I...I haven't been on a date for...for a very long time. And leaving for a date from my parents' house is..."

Keaton grabs my hand gently. "You don't need to explain. Let's have a nice dinner, yes?"

I shake my head in agreement. "I'd like that."

"And you look beautiful, Rosi."

Keaton opens the passenger side car door of his red Honda—not his work truck. I watch him walk back to his side of the car. His dark brown hair is slicked back with a bit of gel but not too much. He wears clean khakis and a long-sleeve button down light blue shirt.

"Why are you smiling?" he asks when he gets in the car.

"You clean up well."

"I do use a shower," he laughs.

"Of course you do. I just meant I'm used to seeing you at work behind a bar or digging in the dirt."

"And is my job too disgusting for your liking?" he laughs.

"Not at all! I like you dirty!" I throw my hand over my mouth the minute the words escape my mouth. "I mean…I mean I like you clean *or* dirty. Well, that's not much better. Let me try…"

After Keaton starts the car, he leans over and kisses my neck. "I think I might like you dirty, too."

I punch his arm. "You're rotten. Can we *please* drive to the restaurant and restart this awkward conversation?"

The Italian restaurant Keaton has chosen overlooks the 18th tee next to a beautiful lake on the south side of Tucson Valley. It's warm enough to eat outside, but we choose a table with a large window looking onto the golf course.

"What are you thinking?" Keaton asks after we are seated.

"I think I might try the lasagna." I hold the menu closer to my face as I didn't bring my reading glasses.

"I don't mean what are you thinking about the menu. I mean what are you thinking about this evening?"

"Our date?" I smile, setting the menu next to my plate. "I think it's nice to get to know you better. But I'm going back to Illinois next week, so I really don't think a second date makes much sense."

"You are presumptive to think I'd want a second date."

"Oh! Right. Sorry, I just meant…"

Keaton smiles so kindly that my heart melts despite my embarrassment. "You are really too easy to tease, Rosisophia Doroche Laruee. I already knew I wanted a second date before I left my house for our first date."

"Let's see how you feel at the end of the evening."

The waiter returns to take our order. I choose white wine with my lasagna and a side salad with Italian dressing. Keaton orders pasta primavera and a side salad with bleu cheese dressing. The tables continue to fill in. I'm glad we made reservations.

"How long have you been living in Tucson Valley?" I ask after taking a long sip of wine.

"I grew up in Nogales, which is about an hour and a half south of here. My dad worked construction, and my mom taught English to immigrant children. She'd been a missionary in Mexico during college when she met my dad. She was a New Jersey girl, and she stood out with her big personality and big '80s hair from the looks of the old pictures. She was 20 when she met my dad. He was 24. He started attending church where she was working, but I don't really think it was God who he was willing to convert for. They kept in touch as pen pals for a year. When she came back the next summer he proposed. It shocked my East Coast grandparents, but no one could deny how crazy he was for her. So, long story short, they got married and moved to Southern Arizona. Dad became a US citizen a couple of years later, my three older sisters were born, and then my parents' dream came true when a perfect, eight pounds, bouncing bundle of joy was born!"

"You?" I ask, laughing.

"Yours truly."

"And are your parents still living in Nogales?"

Keaton's eyes fall as he takes a long sip of his beer before speaking. "My mom was killed in a car crash in Mexico when they were visiting my aunt and uncle eleven years ago."

"Oh my God!"

"Dios Mio indeed. That was a hard one to accept."

I put my hand on top of Keaton's hand. "I can't imagine."

"That's okay. You're not supposed to imagine something like that. Dad moved back to Mexico to be near his siblings. My marriage took a hit, though. My ex-wife tried to *fix* me, and I just wanted to be left alone to grieve.

We ended up fighting more than loving. But I've had a lot of good counseling. I'm where I'm supposed to be now."

"Wow."

"And now that the cold, hard facts are out there about Keats, what about you, Rosi? What's your story?"

Before I can answer, I am drawn to a couple sitting in a corner booth at the far end of the restaurant. "Huh. Look at that. But don't really look because then they'll know we are staring," I say as I stop Keaton from turning around by putting my hand on his shoulder.

"Can you tell me at least? The suspense is killing me."

"Bob is on a date, it seems, with Karen."

"That's a good thing, right? I mean, Bob lost someone he loved, and it's healthy to move forward—something that took me a long time to realize."

"I agree." I stare at Bob and Karen but think about Wes and me and how long ago that now seems when we were happy, well before he took up the hobby of sleeping with Cara in our bed. I just didn't see it at the time. I'd been too busy raising a child and covering other people's hot messes around Springfield.

"Rosi? Is there something wrong?"

I shake my head back and forth. "No. In fact, there's a whole lot of something right...for Bob, I mean," I smile coyly.

"You are a hard one to figure out sometimes." Keaton puts his hand on top of mine and rubs his finger along my skin. It tickles, but I don't want him to stop.

"Here you go!" The waiter sets our plates of food in front of us. "Would you like another drink?"

"Sure."

"I'll pass," says Keaton. "Someone has to get this little lady home safely.

I am thinking how nice it is to have someone concerned about my safety as I cut a piece of lasagna when Keaton suddenly stops eating. "Ah-oh," he says.

"What's the matter?"

"Now it's my turn to tell you not to turn around, but Officer Daniel just walked in. He's talking to a woman at a table over there." He nods his head behind me. The woman looks angry.

"I don't care. I have to look." I not-so-subtly turn around in my chair. I am not the only one straining their necks to get a look because the conversation between Officer Daniel and the woman is getting louder. Officer

Daniel is wearing his uniform. Does this man ever take it off? I can't see who he is talking to, so I toss my spoon onto the floor past our table.

"What are you doing?" Keaton asks, his eyes widening in surprise.

"Oops! Silly me!" I get up to retrieve my spoon. And then I get a clear view of the woman that Officer Daniel is talking to.

My hand is shaking when I sit down again. I wish I could duck under the table and hide.

"What's wrong, Rosi? Who's the woman?"

"It's Officer Kelly," I whisper.

"Who?"

"Office Kelly. Officer Daniel's partner."

"Why is that such a big deal?"

"Because I gave Officer Daniel some information today that might get Officer Kelly arrested."

"Arrested? A police officer? For what?"

"For theft. Or murder."

I fill Keaton in on my observations of Officer Kelly and my conversation with Officer Daniel. He listens intently, leaning in closer so as not to miss a single detail while at the same time keeping a watchful eye on the table behind us.

"Whoa! That is quite a story." He runs a hand through his thick hair, and somehow every strand of hair lies down in the same perfect spot as before he touched his head.

"Are they still there?" I ask, considering moving my chair to Keaton's side of the table.

"Yes, but Officer Kelly's dinner companion isn't at the table anymore."

"Where did he go?"

"Do you want me to see if he's in the bathroom and get some intel?"

I smile. Sleuthing with a partner is a lot more fun. I'm used to working a story for the paper all alone in my office or while driving to interview leads. I miss my job. What job, though? I have no job to go back to. "No. I won't make you go that far. But thanks."

"Uh-oh. Officer Daniel is pointing at you. And Officer Kelly looks ticked."

The desire to hide under the table returns. "What do you think I should do?"

"Finish your lasagna. It's getting cold."

"Good idea. It's really none of my business, anyway, is it?"

"Maybe it should be. No one else seems as interested in finding Salem's murderer. Officer Daniel knew nothing about the counterfeit book angle and the number of suspects Salem's illegal activities might bring up, and Officer Kelly has secrets she's keeping for whatever immoral reason," Keaton pauses. "Don't look now, but Officer Daniel is on his way over to our table."

I take a bite of my salad and wait.

"Excuse me, Rosi? Hello, Keaton."

"Oh, Officer Daniel, what a surprise to see you here tonight. Are you dining in?" Keaton kicks me under the table, and I try not to laugh.

"I…uh…I was here on official business." He glances at Keaton trying to read whether he knows everything I know or not. "Could you meet me tomorrow morning at the…at the place we talked about meeting each other in town?"

"Yes, I can do that. 10:00?"

"That will be fine. Thanks. Have a good night."

This time I turn around to watch Officer Daniel escort Officer Kelly and her companion—who has returned to the table—out of the restaurant. Nobody looks happy.

The waiter returns with a large piece of tiramisu and two forks. "Enjoy your dessert," he says happily.

"We didn't order dessert," I say.

"That gentleman over there paid for your dessert." He points at Bob. "Enjoy."

I wave at Bob who is smiling. He and Karen wave back. "That was really ni…" I can't finish my sentence because Keaton is putting tiramisu into my mouth with a fork. "Wow," I say when I am done with the first bite. "That's delicious." I begin to giggle. I giggle so hard that I have to throw my hand over my mouth so I don't make too much noise.

"What on earth are you laughing about?" Keaton's eyes twinkle as a smile spreads across his face.

"You stabbed my gum with the fork, and now all I can do is taste blood."

"Oh no! I am so sorry, Rosi. I am so stupid. I don't know why I try these things." He hands me a fresh napkin from the middle of the table.

"No! Please don't stop. No one has ever fed me dessert before. I…hiccup…oops! I think it was a very sweet…hiccup…gest…ure." I take a long drink of my wine, hoping to calm the hiccups, but it doesn't work.

By the time we have finished dessert, taking no more stabbing chances, my hiccups have diminished. Bob and Karen don't stop at our table as they leave through the back door, hand in hand. It's sweet. Karen has been described as mousy in looks with her unkept hair and bland-colored clothes, but what she may lack in looks she makes up for in the sweetest of personalities. Maybe Bob has finally realized that someone other than a person with a showy shell like Salem is worth dating.

"I'll get the next bill," I say as Keaton pays for the bill using the credit card machine at the table.

"So, can we definitively establish that there *will* be a second date?"

"I'm going back to Illinois, Keats. I'd love for there to be a second date. I just don't know how much sense it makes." My heart sinks as I say the words aloud.

"Come on. Let's go see Barley. I'm sure she misses you."

"Does that mean you are inviting yourself over to *my parents' house*?" I ask as if I am sixteen again.

"I am most definitely doing just that." He takes my hand as we walk toward the car. Before he opens the door for me, he leans down until he is looking right into my eyes. I can smell his woodsy aftershave. I close my eyes and inhale the memory. "Do me one favor, Rosi."

Anything is exactly what I want to say in this moment, but I know better. "What's that, Keats?"

"Don't think about next week just yet. Take one moment at a time. Can you do that for me?"

"I can try," I whisper. Then we kiss, in the parking lot of the Italian restaurant. The Arizona heat is elevated on this February night, and it's not because of the black asphalt we are standing on.

Chapter 27

I wake up with a smile on my face for the first time in a very long time. Keaton and I had stayed outside with Barley until well after midnight. We talked more about his family, the fact that he'd been spoiled as the baby in the family and the only boy. His love for baseball. His love for spicy foods. His love for the Arizona Diamondbacks. I talked about Zak. And about my love for reporting news. I told him about why I'd lost my job. He had just listened with no judgment. I told him that I was both terrified of being alone and also empowered. We'd held hands. He'd stroked my leg. We'd cuddled together under a blanket Mom had brought out to us before she went to bed. I'd rested my head against his chest and we'd kissed. A lot. I felt like I was sixteen again. It was exhilarating. Barley sat on his lap, and for a moment I felt like we were a family with our puppy.

I pick up my phone to see a notification from the airline, one more week until my flight back to Illinois. Talk about a buzz kill. I don't know if I'm cut out to weather the ups and downs of my rollercoaster of emotions during my time in Tucson Valley. But I don't have time to think because I'm supposed to meet Officer Daniel at Salem's Stories this morning.

There's a note from Mom on the refrigerator that I see when I am looking for the orange juice.

Taken your dad to WATCH his friends play golf. See you for lunch if you are around. Left you the car. Richard is our ride.

I smile. I knew Dad couldn't stay away from the golf course no matter what the doctors told him. After a quick shower, I change into jeans and a red hoodie. It had been chilly this morning when I let Barley outside to pee.

I put Barley in her dog bed in my bedroom, but before I close the door, I make the mistake of looking at her one last time. Her puppy dog eyes are so sad. She knows I'm leaving. She's a very smart dog. She whimpers so pathetically it reminds me of when Zak was a baby and I'd cave every time he cried in his crib and picked him up despite all the evidence from experts to let him cry it out.

"You are hopeless!" I grab the leash from my dresser, attach it to Barley's collar, and let her follow me to the car. She has a complete attitude adjustment by the time I'm sitting in the driver's seat, her tongue hanging out of her mouth as she pants with excitement. I hope Officer Daniel likes dogs.

Officer Daniel is waiting outside Salem's Stories when I park my parents' car in front. He's wearing jeans and a black hoodie. I'm taken aback seeing him look so *human*.

"Hello, Rosi." He stares at Barley.

"Barley," I say. "I hope it's okay that I brought her. She's spent time in the store before, so I thought I could keep her out of the way."

"Yeah, sure. It's fine." His shoulders hang low, and a sense of sadness emanates from every part of his body.

"Are you okay, Officer Daniel?" I ask.

"Dan."

"Okay, Dan. Is there a reason you aren't wearing your uniform?"

"It was a rough night. The sheriff came into the office this morning and told me I could take the day off."

"Oh. Does that mean that…?"

"That Morgan was arrested? Yep. I still can't believe it. I've gone over and over my time with her to see if I missed something, but I still can't find a lapse in my judgment. She was an exemplary officer. I trained her myself. The only thing that struck me as odd was her incessant amount of smiling," he sighs.

I reach for the key under the flower box where I'd returned it in a hurry after my quick escape from Barry. Barley barks excitedly, presumably remembering the place where she'd spent so much of her early weeks with her brothers and sisters. Officer Daniel locks the door behind us.

"Do you have a motive as to why Officer Kelly killed Salem?"

"What? I never said she murdered Ms. Mansfield!" Officer Daniel rubs his temples as if my question has seriously disturbed him.

"I thought that's…"

"We had a warrant to check her house after I followed up on your lead about the jewelry at the pawn shop. We found a lot more jewelry in the house. She confessed to selling Ms. Mansfield's jewelry, but she didn't steal it."

"But how did she get the jewelry?"

"Salem bribed her."

Now I am the one who is confused.

Officer Daniel sighs. "It's so messed up, Rosi. You know that counterfeit theory you shared about Salem selling forged books?" I nod my head. "Officer Kelly investigated the reports from disgruntled customers while I was out of town at my grandmother's funeral. I never knew about the reports. Salem begged her to keep quiet. She offered her the jewelry in exchange for keeping the complaints quiet and ignoring her forgery operation."

"Wow. What I don't understand is why Officer Kelly would jeopardize her career by taking the bribe."

"Do you remember that man who was with her last night at the restaurant?"

"Yes."

"That's her high school boyfriend. He lives in Nebraska, and apparently Officer Kelly wanted to move him to Arizona. He's a bum with no job. I don't know what she sees in that loser. Anyway, she said she was desperate to do anything to get extra money to move him here and buy a house together—the American dream, I guess?" He stares absently past me as if he still can't believe it's true.

"That's an incredible story."

"I still can't believe I judged her character so poorly."

"Hey, don't blame yourself. She's the one that took the bribe, not you. Money is a funny motivator for all sorts of things. But you're sure she didn't have anything to do with Salem's murder?"

"I don't think so. She's greedy, but she's not a murderer, but what do I know? Actually, I do know. I checked our calendar. She was investigating a car break-in case with me outside the library the morning of Salem's murder. Her alibi is me." He exhales slowly.

I pat Officer Daniel on the back because I don't want to hug him, but the poor man needs some kind of physical connection. "Shall we see if we can find the information that Barry was looking at on the computers? About the counterfeit books? Maybe we will get more clues?"

"Yes, that's exactly what I want to do. Thanks, Rosi. I'm glad you're here."

This time I don't feel repulsed. Officer Daniel isn't the slimy character I'd thought him to be. He's only an insecure man trying to promote more confidence on the outside than he's really feeling on the inside. Is that really different from what the rest of us are doing?

I let Barley loose in the store while Officer Daniel and I try to access the desktop computer behind the counter. The computer has been turned off, so now we have to find a password. We pull open drawers and skim through papers, post-it notes, anything that might have a password. We try so many combinations of words and names and numbers that we find that the computer times out. "Now what?" he asks.

"Let's take a break. I want to see the back office." We walk toward the office where I plan to show Officer Daniel all of the things Mom had purchased for Salem's counterfeiting antics, though I have no intention of telling him about Mom's involvement. However, we are distracted by Barley's barking.

"Barley! Barley, no!" Barley stands on the spot where I'd found Salem's body. The floor is wet.

"Did she pee?"

"I don't understand. She never pees in the house. I took her out before we left." I walk toward the puddle and realize something I hadn't considered the day I found Salem's body or the day I'd let myself into Salem's Stories and retraced my steps. "I think Barley was marking her territory."

"What? Why would she do that? There aren't any other dogs here." Officer Daniel scrunches up his nose with confusion and repulsion at the same time.

"I think…I think Salem may have peed before she died? When she died? After she died?"

"Excuse me?"

"There was something wet on the floor when Salem died. And when I came back to look around last week, the spot was still there—not wet anymore of course—but it had an odor that was *familiar*?"

"Well, the body can do *interesting* things when it dies. Are you thinking there's more to that 'situation'?" he asks, making air quotes with his fingers.

"I don't know." I walk toward Barley who is looking quite pleased with herself. "That's where there was blood," I point to the stain on the ground. "I think she hit her head when she fell. And the bathroom is right there."

"So, are you saying Salem was just running to the bathroom because she had to pee so badly that she tripped, hit her head, and died? Because the autopsy didn't say anything about a bleed out from a head wound. There would have been a lot more blood."

"True, but…" I hesitate.

"What, Rosi? Just spit it out."

"The rumor is that poison was found in Salem's system. Is that true?"

"Some elements of Ms. Mansfield's toxicology report and autopsy were irregular, but there were no definitive findings or evidence of narcotics or alcohol. But that doesn't eliminate the theory that someone tried to poison her. The coroner indicated that we couldn't eliminate that theory, so we've been kind of focused on poisoning as a cause of death, but when you don't know what poison you are looking for, it's tough."

"Hmm…Can we move to her office now?"

"If you take that dog with you so she doesn't mark any more territories."

"Okay." I leash Barley who happily follows us to Salem's office. It's the first time I've been in the space. It's more like a workshop than an office. In fact, there's very little about the space that screams *I'm an office.* There are sponges, ribbons, wax paper boxes, stacks of paper of varying thickness. Assorted books and loose book pages lie scattered in the workplace. I see many of the things Mom had purchased like tea bags to age paper and different-colored ink bottles. There's one item that piques my curiosity the most. I take a tissue from the tissue box and lift the bottle of ammonia. Mom had shared her online research that talked about using ammonia to give paper an aged look. "Early in the investigation you told me that Officer Kelly had found some evidence in Salem's office that may have indicated foul play. What was that evidence?"

"Oh, that? Yeah, it was a bluff. I was trying to get you to spill any gossip that your mother or her friends might have. I was desperate."

"Hmm," I say, recalling Officer Daniel's threat.

He ignores the conversation as he inspects Salem's things. "These are the books Ms. Mansfield was counterfeiting, aren't they?" Officer Daniel asks as he picks up the cover of a *Wizard of Oz* book that is not attached to any pages.

"I think so." I open the ammonia bottle and take a gentle smell from a distance.

"What are you doing, Rosi? That's dangerous."

The smell hits the back of my throat, and I cough, reaching instinctively for the only water bottle on the table, an orange Yeti with stickers of books like *To Kill a Mockingbird* and *Wuthering Heights* along with sayings like *Read, Read, Repeat.* "Yes—DUMB!" I put the water bottle to my lips, awaiting a long drink of water, but it's not water in the bottle. I drop the water bottle automatically the moment I smell the ammonia inside, causing the contents to soak the papers on the worktable.

"Why would you do something so dumb?"

I ignore his question and rush to the bathroom to clear my throat so I will stop coughing. After a few moments at the sink, I return to Officer Daniel who has amassed a handful of paper towels and is about to soak up the contents of Salem's water bottle. "Wait!" I grab his elbow.

"What are you doing?" he asks annoyed.

"Dan, there was ammonia in that water bottle."

"What?"

"It's Salem's water bottle! It has to be Salem's water bottle! I wasn't thinking. Salem's water bottle had ammonia inside. I smelled it. I panicked after taking a baby whiff of it, knowing I was a hot second away from swallowing it!"

"Wait a minute! Salem drank ammonia?" His eyes light up with excitement for the first time this morning. "Is ammonia poisoning a thing?"

"I guess so. Maybe? I don't know. Isn't that something a police officer should know?"

Officer Daniel pulls out his cellphone and chooses a contact. "Hi. Can I speak with Coroner Youngston, please?" He looks at me and nods his head. "I'm on to something, Rosi," he whispers. "Yes, hi, Catherine. I was hoping you could help me with something. Yes, great. Can you pull the toxicology report for Salem Mansfield? Yes, I'll wait."

I glance around the office, wondering about something that had been bugging me. Most every inch of the room is cluttered with something book related or book forgery related. It still surprises me that Officer Daniel didn't notice the counterfeiting supplies upon a search of Salem's Stories after Salem's death, though I suppose it may have been possible to miss if one didn't have some knowledge about such things. Plus, maybe Officer Kelly did a search of the office. She would have had incentive to not mention the counterfeiting venture.

"Yes, thank you. Could you tell me if anything you noted in your findings indicated an elevated level of ammonia in Ms. Mansfield's system? Uh-huh. And is that indicative of ammonia poisoning? Thank you for your time, Catherine. Oh, and can you refresh my memory about anything else that looked unusual in the findings?" He looks at me and smiles. "Thank you. Have a nice day." Officer Daniel pushes the red button on his phone. "Her blood ammonia levels were elevated. And there was also evidence of a larger than normal finding of diuretics in her system."

"The water pill? That might explain why she peed herself. That's good news about the ammonia, right? I mean, that's the cause of death then. Ammonia poisoning?"

"Not exactly. The levels were elevated only slightly. Coroner Youngston said that finding alone doesn't prove ammonia poisoning."

"There's something else I am curious about. You arrested Bob Horace because he was the last person you'd seen come into Salem's Stories before I found Salem's body."

"Yes?"

"You'd indicated that you'd known this from video camera footage, correct?"

"Yes, that's correct."

"And did you remove the video camera?"

"We did."

"Hmm…then how come Barry knew I was in the store that day I caught him looking at his mother's emails?"

"Are you sure he didn't see you while you were still in the store?"

"I'm quite positive, but the graffiti on my parents' car telling me to stop snooping showed up on that night."

"How do you know that it was Barry who spray-painted the message?"

"I...I have a source, but I'd rather not say." I continue talking, so Officer Daniel doesn't have time to ask me any more questions as I have no intention of outing Devin for his involvement with Barry and his schemes. "That makes me suspicious that there is another video camera somewhere in the store."

"Hmm, well, I suppose that's possible. We did a very thorough job investigating, of course, but those cameras get smaller and smaller, you know?"

"Of course," I say convincingly though I don't for a second think that Officer Daniel has handled this investigation with competence.

"Let's take a look."

Officer Daniel and I separate, searching for a hidden video camera. He wanders to the front of the store. I scour the back office first, looking more carefully at all of the items scattered throughout the room: boxes of new books that will never see the shelves, holiday decorations, fancy notebooks with discount stickers, a printout for

244

March's orders, and, of course, all of the items used to counterfeit books—but no camera. I shut Barley behind the front counter with the remaining dog gate and walk toward the back door. It's marked as *emergency exit only* though I imagine there is a parking spot or two in the back for employees as there are other businesses along the street, and I've seen cars parked out back. I glance above the door, and there, not hidden well at all, is a video camera. "I've got it!" I yell to Officer Daniel.

Officer Daniel takes a step ladder from the office and climbs atop to remove the video camera from above the door. "We still have Ms. Mansfield's laptop at the station in evidence. Our tech people will try to pull up any footage like they did from the front door camera that showed Bob Horace enter the store."

"I imagine that Barry will know we've been here today if he is monitoring the security footage from his cellphone, too."

"Good point. I'll speak with him today—after I put my uniform back on, of course."

"Of course," I agree. "I appreciate you letting me come with you today. I didn't know Salem other than as a one-time customer, but I'm curious to find out what happened to her. A lot of people in this town have very strong feelings about her."

"The department has taken a big hit to our reputation because we've been unable to arrest a suspect that makes sense—and that we have evidence to convict. And when news of Officer Kelly's bribery and obstruction in the case gets out, we'll be the laughingstock of Tucson Valley. We need to arrest someone, the *right* someone."

"I understand the need to solve this case quickly."

Officer Daniel stares at me pensively. "You're a good investigator, Rosi. Did you ever think about becoming a police officer?"

I laugh. "No. I'll leave that job to the professionals, like you," I say, blowing up his ego. "But I do like figuring out a good mystery."

"I don't know if we will ever figure out who put the ammonia in Salem's water bottle or if it contributed to her death, but I feel like we may be one step closer."

"Do you suspect that Barry had something to do with Salem's murder?"

Officer Daniel shakes his head. "No, I wish it were that easy. We looked into his whereabouts as well as those of Salem's sister Sparrow and her wife. Both had easy to verify alibis hundreds of miles away. This was a local hit job, although I'm going to follow up on those emails you shared with me from disgruntled customers online. I'm going to ask the county sheriff to come by with the crime scene kit to collect the ammonia bottle and water bottle. I'll be in touch."

"Thanks, Dan. I have every confidence in you," I lie—with a big smile on my face as I lead Barley out of the store.

Chapter 28

"Rosi, there's someone I'd like you to meet," Mom says as I walk into the house with Barley after leaving Salem's Stories.

I'm still processing what we'd found at the bookstore, and I don't really want to visit with anyone. I wave at the woman sitting in my dad's recliner, guessing he's hiding in the backyard. "Excuse me a minute, please." I open the slider and let Barley into the yard before returning to the living room. The woman is likely in her 50s with exceptionally clear skin and a cute curly hairdo that bounces on her head as she's talking excitedly with Mom.

When they see me, the woman stops talking, stands up, and reaches out her hand for me to shake. "Hello, Rosi. I'm Tracy Lake."

"Nice to meet you, Ms. Lake," I say, raising an eyebrow at Mom.

"This comes as a surprise your mom's told me."

"Please sit down, both of you," Mom says. "Tracy and I attend tap class together. She's one of our best tappers—and one of our youngest residents," she laughs.

"It's true. I only *just* qualify to own a house here. I'm 55."

"That's great, but I am not interested in learning tap dance any time soon, and I'm returning to Illinois next week."

"That's why I'm here, not to convince you to tap dance, though." She and Mom share a secret look. "I'd like for you to consider *not* going back to Illinois."

"Excuse me?"

"I am a permanent resident of Tucson Valley Retirement Community, but I have been a resident of Tucson Valley for much of my life. I'm the executive director of the Tucson Valley Retirement Community Senior Center. It's my job to oversee the daily programs and special events, to budget, to keep our residents happy. I need an assistant, someone to oversee the performing arts wing of our community and someone to direct the sales and marketing team for the retirement community—well, I use the term *team* loosely—because really this person is only directing themself." She puts her hand to her mouth and giggles. "Your mom has told me about your background in media, and I'd like to offer you the job."

Both women stare at me. I'm too stunned to speak for a moment.

"Isn't that great news, Rosi? Now you have a job, and you can stay here with Dad and me as long as you'd like. And even when we go back to Illinois, we know you'll be here when we return in a few months! It's a wonderful solution."

"I...I really hadn't planned on staying in Arizona, Ms..."

"Tracy," she says.

"I realize this is a surprise. I've put together a package for you to consider." She hands me a file folder with papers inside. "We offer a hybrid position with only three days a week in the office required, healthcare with vision and dental, membership to the sports complex even though you'd normally be too young to join, and discounted tickets to any of our programs. It's a great package. The management at Tucson Valley Retirement Community knows the value of planning for your future. They take care of their employees which is part of the reason I took this job, and, of course, the people are pretty amazing." She squeezes Mom's knee. Mom looks like she might burst with excitement.

I inhale deeply. "That is a great offer."

"The salary is nice, too." She points to the folder. "You'll see the details inside."

"Thanks. I will take a look and get back with you, Tracy. Please excuse me, but I have an appointment I need to tend to."

"Of course. Please be in touch." We shake hands again, and I escape to the backyard where the only appointment I have is to clear my head.

"Mom's at it again, isn't she?" asks Dad. He is sitting in the shade under the umbrella of the table. Barley is sitting on his lap.

"Will she ever stop meddling?" I sink into the chair next to him. Barley doesn't give me any notice.

"I wouldn't hold my breath."

We sit in silence for a long time. Mom knows better than to come into the backyard right now. A hummingbird hovers over the orange flowers of a butterfly bush at the edge of the yard. Keaton taught me the names of all the plants in the backyard: calendula, hibiscus, prickly pear cactus. It's hard not to think about Keaton when considering an offer to stay in Arizona, but nobody should choose a new place to live based upon a good first date.

That's insane. Still, I need a job, and the offer is good. I've perused the papers inside the file folder.

Finally, Dad shoos Barley from his lap and gets up. With slow steps he walks back toward the house. He pats me on the head as he passes by. "You'll do the right thing, Rosi. You are welcome wherever you land. Don't forget that."

Chapter 29

The Tucson Valley Retirement Community claims to host the largest classic car show in the state of Arizona. The event will bring thousands of people into the little community, and specifically, into the retirement community limits. The Mabel Brown Sports Complex, senior center, and performing arts auditorium parking lots will feature the cars participating in the event with a $1000 best in show and a $500 runner-up prize being awarded. Dad is as giddy as a child going to their first major league baseball game.

"You'd better take your walker, Richard. There are going to be a lot of people shuffling around today."

"I know, Renee. I know what I'm doing. It's not my first car show in Tucson Valley, you know?"

Dad is sporting a cowboy hat, and I try not to laugh when I see him. But he reads my mind.

"It offers the best sun protection, Rosi. Don't judge."

"You do you, Dad."

"Thanks again for your help today, Rosi. We need every helper we can get. It's going to be crazy. Plus, it's warm. That means our volunteers will need to cycle in and out of the sun. We don't need anyone dropping because of heat exhaustion," says Mom who is wearing a sleeveless lime green sundress and floppy cream hat.

"I think people can handle eighty degrees, Mom, if they can handle 110 degrees in the summer."

"You're wrong, Rosi. Most of the people here are snowbirds, like us. They don't stay here year-round."

"Are you two done yapping? I want to get there when they open the parking lots. It's going to be crowded."

My parents weren't kidding. Even at opening time, there are hundreds and hundreds of people in every direction. Shiny cars, polished up, reflecting the sun. Hoods open to show off souped-up engines. Cruisers, classics, and sports cars. I don't even care much about cars, and I am excited to walk between the rows.

"I'm going to meet Frank," Dad says as he grabs hold of his walker.

"Ugh. That poor man, married to someone as rude as Jan. Of course he'd have a car in the running for best of show."

"Mom, when did you change your opinion about Jan?"

"After she and her dreadful nephew treated you so poorly, Rosi. No one treats my daughter like that and expects me not to notice."

I put my arm around my mom. "Let's find those raffle tickets we're supposed to be selling."

Karen, Paula, and Brenda wave at Mom and me when they see us. I wonder if Brenda has "forgiven" me for dismissing her pickleball partner, more like *prickleball*. Allen is so distasteful. The Tucson Valley Retirement Community Senior Center is selling 50-50 raffle tickets with half of the proceeds going to them and half going to the winning raffle ticket owner. When Mom is comfortably set up with her friends (why exactly did she need my help?), I pay a visit to the beer tent. It doesn't open until noon, but Keaton's organizing the setup crew. The same crew that worked the bar at karaoke night is working here today. I find him tying the tents to stakes in the ground adjoining the sports' complex parking lot.

"Hey, cutie," he says when he sees me walking his direction. I'm wearing a white eyelet tank top and red shorts. I'm glad I remembered to put on lip gloss this morning.

"Hi, Keats. Even you are wearing shorts today!"

"You might need your shades."

"Huh?" I ask, wrinkling my forehead.

"Because these legs are h-o-t—hot!" He throws his head back in laughter.

"Funny." It's so easy being with Keaton. He's uncomplicated and real. What you see is what you get. I could get used to spending more time with him.

"Give me a second to finish up, and I'll walk to the opening ceremonies with you."

"Opening ceremonies?"

"It's a tradition. The mayor welcomes everyone. The rules for voting are announced, and for kicks, all of the participants honk their horns at the same time. It's quite an auditory treat!" he smiles.

"Well, we can't miss that, can we?"

I hold the tent flap while Keaton pounds the last stake into the ground. "All done. This tent isn't going anywhere. Plus, we've got two hours to spend together until the beer starts flowing."

We walk hand in hand to the stage where Mayor Kettleman is walking to the podium. We join the onlookers who seem eager to hear his opening remarks so that the festivities can begin. Mom joins us from her most important job, everything seeming to pause at this moment as the crowd converges to welcome the beginning of the Tucson Valley Retirement Community Classic Car Show.

"Last year Salem was on that stage with Troy," Mom whispers, "even though she was seeing Bob. She was wearing a ridiculous fur coat and boots that went up to her knees. But he was smitten. He even tripped on his way to the podium because he couldn't keep his eyes off her. The crowd went wild. And do you know what Salem did? She just shook her head back and forth with a scowl as if she were embarrassed to know him. What these men saw in her I will never know."

"Ladies and gentlemen, I'd like to welcome you to the fifteenth annual Tucson Valley Retirement Community Classic Car Show. Woo-Wee, try saying that ten times!"

The crowd laughs.

"He says that every year," Mom says, but she's laughing along with the crowd anyway.

"Cowboy Donnie will lead us in prayer, or a moment of silence—your choosing." He steps away from the podium. The crowd bows their heads.

"Dearly Beloved..."

But I don't follow the prayers of Cowboy Donnie because I don't have my eyes closed. I'm following the movement of one man who is moving closer and closer to the stage as if he has a purpose with each step he takes.

"And the crowd said…"

"Amen!"

Officer Daniel stands next to Troy Kettleman who has frozen into his place on the stage, all eyes on the two of them.

"What is happening?" Mom and Keaton are whispering in each of my ears.

"I'm not sure, but it can't be good—for Troy."

Jan seizes the moment as hers and walks onto the stage, followed by Frank. He grabs the microphone before she can which clearly irritates her as she tries, unsuccessfully, to grab it back. "Please, car owners, on the count of three, honk…those…horns. Everyone ready?"

The crowd applauds, hoots, and hollers. Officer Daniel and the mayor take a step back.

"One. Two. Three!" yells Frank. A chorus of horns toot, squeak, squawk, and wail for a full ten seconds. Jan says something, too, but no one hears her. The festivities have begun.

While most of the crowd disperses to view the classic cars, the locals stay put, moving closer to the stage until they are as close to it as possible without actually climbing atop. I may not be local, but I have to suspect that Officer Daniel's appearance has something to do with Salem's death.

Officer Daniel walks closer to the podium, the microphone still on. He looks side-eye at the crowd of onlookers before turning back to Troy. "Troy Kettleman, you are under arrest for the murder of Salem Mansfield," he projects over the crowd, the taking back of his honor and respect from a community of people that thought him an incompetent buffoon.

Troy makes no protestations as if he'd been waiting for this moment. He holds his head and wipes his eyes with his fingers. "I didn't mean to hurt her. I only wanted her to fall ill—to beg for me to help her. *To need me.* To need me and not Bob. She wasn't supposed to die." He looks out at the audience who all stare at him with distaste. It's one thing to dislike someone like Salem Mansfield, but it's quite another to support her murder.

"Wow!" Brenda says aloud. Mom shoots her a dirty look.

Officer Daniel leads Mayor Kettleman off the stage in handcuffs. Bob, standing next to Karen, glares at him with nothing but hatred on his face.

"Excuse me a minute," I say, following a few steps behind Officer Daniel until he has shut Troy into the back of his police car. "Dan!"

He turns around and smiles when he sees me. "Hi, Rosi. That was something, huh?" He beams with pride and narcissism, but I don't mind so much right now.

"But how did you know? Was there something on the tape?"

"Troy entered through the back door ten minutes after Bob left through the front door, but Salem never knew he was there. The camera shows him entering the office with a bottle that looked like bleach and exiting five minutes later. You and all of Tucson Valley just heard him confess that he didn't 'mean' for Ms. Mansfield to die. The coroner and I went over the ammonia blood levels again. While she reinforced that the ammonia alone wasn't enough to kill her, the combination with the bleach inside her water bottle may have produced a toxic gas called chloramine."

"And she was found near the bathroom."

"Trying to get to fresh water and to get the taste of ammonia and bleach out of her mouth just like you tried to wash out the *smell* from the ammonia bottle in her office."

"But she got light-headed or sick or whatever from the toxic gas, peed herself from too many diuretics as she was running to the bathroom, fell, and hit her head. Poor thing was just trying to get to the bathroom!"

"What a horrible way to die."

"It really is," I say, looking at Troy in the backseat of Officer Daniel's car. He appears to be sobbing and talking to himself.

"I'm pretty sure he's going to confess everything," Officer Daniel says looking at him.

"I think you're right. Do you believe that he didn't want to kill her?"

"From the toxicology reports, there was only a little bit of ammonia and a little bit of bleach," he says. "I'm guessing he panicked and thought that putting the bleach in the water bottle might make Salem sick enough to need medical attention and that she'd call him for help. The addition of the ammonia may have been a quick decision when he saw the bottle on her desk. It's not like Troy knew there'd be a bottle of ammonia in Salem's office. Being dumped makes people do stupid stuff for attention."

"That's the truth," I shudder, recalling my reaction to Wesley's affair.

"It's the fall that may have done her in. Coroner Youngston re-evaluated her brain images and found evidence of internal bleeding."

"That's what sealed her fate. Huh. Ironic, isn't it?"

"What's that, Rosi?"

"It's ironic that her own books which she clearly loved—both the real ones and the fake ones—contributed to her death when she tripped over them trying to get to the bathroom because she ingested ammonia which she was using to counterfeit books. I believe she was even carrying some of those forged books with her as she ran to the bathroom. I found a couple of books on the ground that seemed out of place."

"Truly ironic. Sometimes a person comes into the world with a wail and leaves the world quietly. And sometimes it's the other way around. I need to get Mr. Kettleman to the police station. If the court is kind, he may just be charged with manslaughter and not first-degree murder. He's pretty torn up inside." He points to Mayor

Kettleman who is rocking back and forth in his seat. "Thanks again for your help."

"You're welcome."

"And Rosi?"

"Yes?"

"I'm glad you'll be staying in Tucson Valley."

"What do you mean?"

"I heard you took a new job." He winks at me and closes his car door to drive back to the station.

"But I didn't…" He is long gone before I can finish my sentence.

Keaton and I drink beer in the beer tent as we watch Jan hold up the trophy for Frank's best-in-show win. She's dripping with pride, and Frank looks pretty stoked, too. Dad is slapping Frank on the back, and Mom is making her amends with Jan by standing nearby for support. Sometimes you have to do those kinds of things when you live in a community where everybody knows everybody. At least she has friends like Karen and Paula, too. Bob and Karen hold hands behind my parents, most likely laughing at something silly my dad has said.

"What are you thinking?" Keaton asks. His eyes reflect the bright sun hitting the hot pavement.

"Oh, I was just wondering what it's like to live in Arizona in the middle of summer."

Keaton laughs. "It's kind of like the front porch of hell."

"That's what I figured."

"Does that mean you might take the job, Rosi?" He flips my hair behind my shoulder and waits expectantly for my answer.

"It's a consideration. I want to talk to Zak, make sure he's comfortable with Mom being a thousand miles away. He's living three hours away from Springfield doing his own thing with work and college now. I don't know how much more I'd see him if I lived in Springfield. But I have to get out of my parents' house. I can't turn forty and still be shacking up in their spare bedroom."

"I've got a spare room," he winks at me.

"Ha! Slow down, stranger. Let's flesh a few more skeletons out of each other's closets first."

"Fair." He stares at me for a long time, but it makes me feel safe, like someone is watching out for me.

"What are *you* thinking?" I finally ask.

"I think your name fits you perfectly."

"Okay. That's an odd thing to say, *Keaton*."

"I'm serious," he smiles. "You are smart like Dorothy, sweet like Rose, sarcastic like Sophia, and sssseeexxxxyyyy like Blanche," he draws out.

"I think the heat is getting to you."

"I don't think so. I can take the heat. The question is, can you?"

"We shall see." I lean my face close to Keaton's where I find his lips with mine and kiss them hard. "Here's to new beginnings."

"Cheers!"

We lift our beers and clink our plastic cups.

The Tucson Valley Retirement Community Cozy Mystery Series

Dying to Go (Nothing to Gush About)

Dying For Wine (Seeing Red)

Dying For Dirt (All Soaped Up)

Dying to Build (Nailed It)

Chapter 1 from Dying For Wine (Seeing Red)

"You're off key! Can't you hear yourself?" screams Sherman Padowski, his toupee moving back and forth as he shakes his fist in anger.

Clyde Andrews, the target of his rage, rolls his eyes in irritation at the man who looks a lot like him save for the toupee on Sherman's head. Clyde has his own hair combed neatly and greased back in the vein of a 1960s Filly Sinclair hairstyle. And since they are both Filly Sinclair impersonators, it makes sense that they'd bear a resemblance.

"Can't you go down an octave?" asks Sherman, frustrated that he's having to give singing advice to someone that makes a living singing, like himself.

It's time to step in. My new job encompasses way more than doing the marketing and social media for

Tucson Valley Retirement Community. I can't be angry, though. Is anyone ever completely honest when it comes to listing the job responsibilities of an open position? There is usually a reason why the position became available to begin with, and it's not always because a completely satisfied employee married the woman of his dreams and had to leave his beloved job. Sometimes there are unfortunate responsibilities that nobody tells you about. And breaking up disputes between the headliners in the 1960s send-off spring concert at the performing arts center is one of those non-disclosed responsibilities.

"Guys! Stop it. You are both professionals," I remind them. "Can't you work out another way to solve your dispute? Maybe sing another song where you are both happy with the octave?" I'd only agreed to having two Sinclair impersonators because Brenda threw such a stink. It turns out that Sherman Padowski is her cousin's wife's brother, and if we didn't let him sing in the 1960s spring extravaganza, then she was boycotting the event and taking all of her friends and their money with her, too. And as much as I despise the plastic woman with a permanent scowl, this event isn't just an entertainment concert event. It's a fundraiser for the performing arts center. We need this event to be a success in order to be able to offer more programs year-round.

"Rosi!"

I turn toward the woman that is yelling my name, but she's only trying to get my attention with her booming voice. She's a docile soul. "I'm coming, Tracy!"

"There you are, Rosi. I need a final count for the concert attendees. There's a waiting list, and I need to know if there are any cancellations I can give away to those waiting. This has never happened before. We've never had a waiting list. I hate to turn people away because it's like throwing guaranteed money out the window, but we only have so many seats. Your marketing campaign has been brilliant, Rosi, just brilliant. How you got JJ McMeadows to emcee our concert was a stroke of genius. The amount of lusting the women in my tap dance class have expressed over that man would curl your toes. If you could hear the things they've said. And I'm the baby in the class at 55." She laughs, a pleasing belly laugh that endears her to anyone who crosses her path.

Tracy is the best boss I have ever worked for. I know it's not politically correct to have worried about working for a female boss, but all of my other bosses have been male. And even though the last one fired me from the Springfield Gazette, I really couldn't hold it against him because he'd learned about the tires I'd slashed on my then-husband's mistress's car. He'd been a good boss, though, and gave me a lot of latitude to cover stories the way I wanted to tell them in Illinois's capital city. But Tracy tops even that boss. She's kind and personable. And trusting.

She's unorganized and forgetful, too. That makes me the perfect addition to the team, as she refers to us. She leads with the glowing personality, and I finish with the organization and details. We have a great lineup of shows and events planned, but this concert will be a farewell event of sorts for the snowbirds who will leave Arizona for the summer and go back to their homes to spread out around the country. Mom and Dad are going back to Illinois soon, too.

"I'll check my messages, but I don't know of any cancellations. Maybe we can add a row of seats in the back of the auditorium behind the row of stadium seats. I think that would allow eight or ten more seats. What do you think?"

"Have Mario take some chairs into the auditorium and guesstimate how many would fit comfortably. And check the fire code to make sure we won't be overcapacity if we add seats. The last thing we need is for this show to be shut down because of a fire code violation. Oh me, oh my, the women in this community would never forgive me! Or, the men, either, for that matter. There are just as many men geeking out over JJ McMeadow's upcoming appearance."

"Dance craze. It's a dance craze, baby. Follow me on the dance floor." Tracy sings aloud as she twirls around the auditorium to JJ MaMeadow's 1965 hit single. Neither of us were alive then, but the song is catchy, and several of the people I've run into since the announcement of JJ's participation in our event have shared their personal stories of seeing JJ perform when they were in their teens. They always have smiles on their faces when they tell their stories. Karen, my favorite of Mom's gaggle of gossipy friends, was blushing as she told me about having a first date with her future husband Albert when he kissed her on the lips as JJ sang "Teenage Lover." Karen and Albert had been married for fifty years before he died three years ago. Now she's "enjoying time" with Bob Horace, as she puts it. And I'm hoping that even though the concert may be bittersweet for her, she can find joy again.

"Forward me the information about the waiting list. I'll take care of that issue. You've got other things to attend to. I hear the lines at the new pickleball court were painted incorrectly."

Tracy rolls her eyes. "You have no idea what a mess those new courts have been. A three-inch discrepancy has driven the diehards mad."

I stifle a giggle.

"Thanks. I'll take you up on your offer. You're a godsend, Rosi, an absolute godsend. There are too many balls in the air for one person to manage the social activities at all of our facilities here in Tucson Valley. I'm grateful that the board *finally* agreed to let me hire another person after Teddy left six months ago. It's been a nightmare keeping the swimmers and the pickleballers and the artists and the actors and the card players and the…"

I put a hand on Tracy's arm. She's spiraling. "Get a fresh coffee. I've got this."

She nods her head, takes a deep breath, and spins down the hallway as she sings "Dance Craze" to herself on the way back to her office.

Back in my office, I settle at my desk which overlooks the parking lot of the Tucson Valley Retirement

Community. It's not a glamorous office with an amazing view, but it beats the cold days of early spring I'd be experiencing back in Illinois. I try not to dwell on what Arizona summers may be like. Barley, my new puppy, jumps onto my lap to interrupt my thoughts. She's getting big quickly, and her Golden Retriever features grow more beautiful every day, even the fur that's constantly flying around her. She's the best thing that's happened to me since my trip to Tucson. It's still hard to admit to myself that my trip to help my parents after Dad's knee replacement surgery has turned into a new permanent residence, a new puppy, and a budding friendship with a hot landscaper. Life after divorce isn't so bad after all. Moving on sounds cliché, but it's truly the best medicine for a broken heart. It doesn't just mean moving on with a new relationship but being willing to try new things. And no one can claim that I haven't tried new things. As if on cue, my office phone rings.

"Hello, this is Rosi Laruee. How may I help you?"

"Hi, Rosi. It's me. Jan."

Barf is what I want to say to my mother's other snooty friend, Jan Jinkins. She and Brenda are two peas in a shriveled-up pod. "Hello, Jan. How may I help you?"

"I'm calling to check on that wait list. Richard and I have tickets, of course, but my sister and brother-in-law, Allen's parents—" she says with emphasis as if I could forget her loathsome nephew who'd made a laughingstock of me at karaoke night when he'd visited his beloved aunt. "are extending their visit just to see JJ McMeadows, and they just *have* to get tickets."

"It is going to be a great night."

"You don't seem to understand, Rosi. They *have* to get tickets. I promised Mary Lou I'd get her those tickets."

"We will do our best to accommodate everyone that wants to attend the concert, Jan. However, we only have so many—"

"Get me those tickets, Rosi. Get me those tickets."

The phone line goes dead.

"Well then, Barley. Perhaps I should check on that waiting list," I sigh. Tracy's agreement to allow me to bring Barley to the office was icing on the cake to an amazing job package. Barley has a way of lowering the temperature of everyone in the office, especially when they have to deal with entitled narcissists like Jan who think that the world should revolve around them. I'd finally asked Mom why she'd chosen Jan and Brenda as friends. "It just kind of happened, Rosi," she'd said. "They came from central Illinois, too, and there is a large contingency of Illinoisians here. I know it's silly, but people tend to form their social groups based upon geography." It made sense to me that the beginnings of relationships might start out that way, but the fact that they *stayed* that way simply because of the state someone had come from seemed pretty dumb. But I didn't tell Mom that, of course.

I open my computer to check my emails. Tracy's updated list has four names of people wanting tickets, not including Allen's parents. No messages or cancellations have come in to me, but two new requests for tickets have arrived, from Sparrow and her wife Tina. Sparrow said she'd be in town to finish the sale of her sister's store and saw the notice about the concert and could I see about getting her tickets? That's a request I am willing to try harder to fill than Allen's parents. I'm so glad that Salem's Stories has a buyer. It'd be a shame to see such a fine bookstore close its doors for good. And now that Salem's murder has been solved, the eeriness of her murder in her own store holds much less mystery.

Barley jumps off my lap and starts barking at the window. I turn around to see Keaton walking through the parking lot to the building. Sometimes I think that Barley loves Keats more than she loves me.

Barley paws at my office door, anticipating Keaton's lunchtime arrival, a new routine we've established: Wednesday lunches together. I pull out a compact mirror from my purse, run my fingers through my long brown hair, and reapply lip gloss so I look casually put together while trying hard not to look like I'm trying hard.

Keaton's face lights up when he sees Barley. His work pants are lightly dirty, but he's put on a clean shirt, I observe, while he squats down to greet Barley. "Hey, girl! How has your day been? The boss treating you okay?" He flashes a smile at me before reaching into his pocket and giving Barley a treat. She licks his hand affectionately. He stands up and walks toward me where I am standing, awaiting his attention next. "Sorry! I didn't bring you a treat!" he laughs.

"Honestly, just seeing you today is treat enough." I accept his kiss. "But don't let that go to your head! I've had some difficult customers today," I say, reaching for my purse. "Can we take Barley and get our food to go? She needs a walk."

"Sure. It sounds like you might need some fresh air, too."

"I do!" I wave goodbye to Tracy in her office and pass by the open door of the auditorium where we are greeted with shouting.

"Clyde, you fool! You're going to screw this whole concert up!"

I peek inside to see Sherman yelling at Clyde. Clyde is standing center stage with a microphone in his shaking hand.

"Do you need to deal with that?" Keaton asks as we spy on the Filly Sinclair impersonators.

"Nope. It can wait. I've discovered that settling disputes between two stubborn, old men isn't a task I'm designed to handle well, *especially* on an empty stomach. Come on. Let's go."

The Secret of Blue Lake (1)

The only true certainty in life is dying, but there's a whole lot of life to live from beginning to end if you're lucky. When Chicago news reporter Meg Popkin's dad makes a surprise move to a tiny town called Blue Lake, Michigan, in the middle of nowhere and away from his family after losing his wife to cancer, she wonders if there is more to the move than *just a change of scenery*. With the help of a new, self-confident reporter at the station, Brian Welter, she tries to figure out what the secret attraction to Blue Lake is for its many new residents and along the way discovers that maybe she's been missing out on some of the joys of living herself.

Drama, mystery, and romance abound for Meg as she learns about love, loss, and herself.

The Secret of Silver Beach (2)

After solving the mystery of the secret of Blue Lake, Meg returns to Chicago and to her new job as co-host on Chicago Midday. But when poor chemistry with Trenton

Dealy leads to problems on the show, Meg is assigned a travel segment that will send her on location all around Lake Michigan visiting beach towns and local tourist attractions. The trip takes her away from fiancé Brian who has to continue anchoring the nightly news in Chicago. When odd threats start hurtling in Meg's direction, she finally confesses to Brian and those closest to her that she might have a stalker. Do the threats have something to do with the new information she learned about her dad's past in the little town of St. Joseph, Michigan, or is there something bigger at play that threatens more than Meg's livelihood?

War and Me

By: Marcy Blesy

Amazon Reviewer: *The story and characters draw you in. I felt like I was in the story and feeling the emotions of each character. I laughed. I cried. I couldn't put the book down! The story takes place during the WW2 era and intertwines love with the realities of war. A must read!*

Flying model airplanes isn't cool, not for fifteen-year-old girls in the 1940's. No one understands Julianna's love of flying model airplanes but her dad. When he leaves to fly bomber planes in Europe forcing Julianna to deal with her mother's growing depression alone, she feels abandoned until she meets Ben, the new boy in town. But when he signs up for the war, too, she has to consider whether letting her first love drift away would be far easier than waiting for the next casualties.

Marcy Blesy is the author of over thirty children and adult books including the popular children's series: EVIE AND THE VOLUNTEERS, NILES AND BRADFORD, THIRD GRADE OUTSIDER, HAZEL, THE CLINIC CAT, and BE THE VET. Her picture book, Am I Like My Daddy?, helps children who have experienced the loss of a parent. Her adult books include cozy mysteries and romance books. By day she teaches creative writing to wonderful students around the world.

Marcy is a believer in love and enjoys nothing more than making her readers feel a book more than simply reading it.

I would like to extend a heartfelt thanks to Betty for being the first person to read Dying to Go (Nothing to Gush About) and for giving me her guidance and expertise as my editor. Thank you to my wonderful friends for being fantastic, encouraging readers of an early draft of this book. I am quite fortunate to have trusted and wise friends who continue this journey with me. Thank you Heather, Keri, Cindy, Kerri, Jill, Stephanie, Kristi, Bette, Suzanne, and Amy!

Thank you to Ed, Connor, and Luke for always championing my dreams.

Printed in Great Britain
by Amazon